MW00944658

The Letter

A Forever Novella

By Darlene Shortridge

Books also by

Darlene Shortridge

The Women of Prayer Series:

Until Forever
Forever Blessed
Forever Loved
(Spring 2013)

The Letter

Copyright © 2013 by Darlene Shortridge. All rights reserved.

No part of this publication may be reproduced, stored in a retrieval system or transmitted in any way by any means, electronic, mechanical, photocopy, recording or otherwise without the prior permission of the author except as provided by USA copyright law.

This novel is a work of fiction. Names, descriptions, entities, and incidents included in the story are products of the author's imagination. Any resemblance to actual persons, events, and entities is entirely coincidental.

Scripture quotations are from the HOLY BIBLE, NEW INTERNATIONAL VERSION®. Copyright 1973, 1978, 1984 Biblica. Used by permission of Zondervan. All rights reserved.

This book is available in print at most online retailers.

Published by DJDM Enterprises

Oklahoma City, Oklahoma 73119

Cover design by Jonna Feavel

Author photo by Photography by Jonna

Published in the United States of America

To my husband,
Daniel John Mawhinney

For his truly is the heart of a
father

Chapter 1
Jessi

Jessi softly returned the phone to its cradle. She knew this day would come although she didn't expect it so soon. She had prepared herself but she still felt some odd stirrings within her that were most unexpected. Truthfully she had thought she would feel nothing.

She sat down at the kitchen table, rested her head in her propped up hands and waited for Mark to come home for lunch. A pot of beef stew was simmering on the stove, thanks to Aunt Merry.

She heard the door creak open and she rose to greet her husband.

Mark turned around, a big smile for her until he saw her red-rimmed eyes. "What's wrong? What happened?"

"Mom just called. Dad had a heart attack. He didn't make it."

Mark wrapped his arms around his wife. "I'm so sorry, honey." He held her and she sobbed on his shoulder. Not because she mourned the man who fathered her, but because she mourned the relationship they never had and would now never have.

* * * *

Mark loaded the last suitcase in the back of the SUV. The twins were in the far back seat playing hand held video games and Aunt Merry and Olivia were sitting in the middle two bucket seats. Jessi climbed into the passenger side and Mark tripped the trip odometer then pulled out of the driveway. "You ready?"

Jessi nodded. "I guess. As ready as I'll ever be."

Impending funeral or not, traveling with a large family was hardly subdued. Bathroom stops and motion sickness eventually gave way to the soft sounds of sleeping children and a slightly snoring aunt. The relative quiet gave Mark and Jessi time to talk about their plans. Jessi's mom had extended an invitation for them all to stay with her. In the past, that would never have been an option. Too many children making too much noise for her impatient father. Now, with her father gone, Jessi had a decision to make.

Being married to the woman sitting next to him for the past fifteen years gave Mark some insight on her thoughts. "I think we need to stay at your mom's place. It'll do you good, give you a chance to talk with her. I think you both need that."

"I know. I just didn't want to give in too soon, you know?"

Mark grinned at his wife. "Still stubborn as ever, huh?"

"That stubbornness has saved our hides more than once I'll have you know."

"I know, and I love you even more because of it."

Jessi called her mom to let her know their plans while Mark pulled into a gas station with a McDonalds attached to it. After rounds of chicken nuggets and cheese burgers Mark found the hotel they normally frequented while making this fourteen-hour drive. Mark and the kids loved it because it had a large indoor pool. Jessi preferred soaking in the hot tub. She always slept better after the jets pounded some of the stress from her tired aching muscles. It was a long drive and the stop halfway helped everyone remain well-mannered passengers.

The next evening Jessi slowly pulled into her mother's driveway. She had never been to this enormous structure of a house her parents had built. The kids scrambled out of the SUV, excitement showing on each of their faces.

Jessi watched her mother step outside, motioning for them all to come in. She turned to Mark. "Here goes nothing."

After helping Aunt Merry from the vehicle, he took his wife's hand and gave her a squeeze. "The Lord's with you, Jessi. I know you. You have too much love to let bitterness keep you from doing what needs done." He stopped and turned her toward him. "You can do this. I believe in you."

Jessi kept quiet. Her thoughts were running the gamut. On one side, she knew her faith gave her no option but to forgive. Forgiveness was everything Christ stood for. On the other side, she'd been hurt and abandoned by these people who were supposed to love her and protect her. Her parents had craved the freedom of being childless even while having a daughter they were responsible for. How could said daughter just open her arms and pretend no wrongs had been done to her? That was the question of the hour.

Jessi allowed herself to be pulled into a hug. Truth be told, there were a few times over the years her mother had been there for her. When Ethan was lying in a coma in the hospital, her mother never left her side. She used to show up for Christmas and bring the greatest gifts. Of course, Jessi now understood her mother was trying to buy her love and apologize for never being around. It worked. At least for the week following Christmas. Afterward she still felt empty inside and lacking somehow. Like something was wrong with her. What kind of parents didn't want anything to do with their kid? Then again, what was so wrong with her that they didn't want to be a part of her life?

She turned her attention to her mother. "You look good."

"Thank you, dear. Your father wouldn't have wanted me to look any other way."

"Yes, of course." Jessi turned, looking for the twins and Olivia. The house was just big enough to get lost in.

"They're fine. Maria is showing them their rooms."

"Oh, okay." Jessi couldn't help but stare at the entryway. She'd fantasized as a young girl about descending a staircase like this one in her wedding gown. "Nice house."

"Thanks. Come on, I'll show you to your room. You have to be exhausted after that drive." Her mother led the way and Mark and Jessi followed with their luggage in hand. Aunt Merry was headed the opposite direction. She'd have to find her after they got settled.

Jessi closed the door and took a quick tour. The room had to have been in the pages of Southern Living Magazine. A four-poster cherry bed with a down comforter and more pillows than any two people could ever use was the focal point of the room. There was a sitting area with two chairs and a table between them. Jessi slowly ran her hand over the soft comforter. *A person could get used to this.*

She opened the drawers to the high boy and unpacked her and Mark's clothing. She was fairly certain she would have the same chore in the twin's room. By now, her mother would be chasing them down. Having two four-year-old boys feeding off one another's energy was a full time job.

Mark pulled her into a hug before they left the comfort of their room. "Hey, I love you."

Jessi nuzzled his neck, trying to enjoy the peace of the moment. She clung to him, both for support and for the comfort his arms offered. She was so thankful she had these arms to fall into.

She pulled away first. "Come on. Let's go see if the kids got settled. And it smells like mom has supper on. I'm hungry."

"That's my girl. You must be getting back to normal if you're thinking of your stomach."

Jessi grabbed one of the pillows from the bed and threw it at him as he ran out the door. She quickly followed on his heels; the enticing smells of supper drawing them closer to the kitchen.

The first thing she thought when entering her mother's kitchen was how Aunt Merry would be in heaven cooking here. The second was, of course Aunt Merry was already at home stirring something in a pot. Figures.

It wasn't long before plates of steaming Mexican food were on the table. Jessi's senses were on overload. Sizzling chicken, beef and shrimp fajitas as well as Spanish rice and Mexican corn cake were all hot and ready to be consumed. The smells were overwhelming.

Jessi pushed back from the table, unable to eat another bite. "Mom, that was delicious. Thank you."

Patty smiled at her daughter. "Well, it's not me you should thank. Maria put this feast together."

Jessi thanked Maria and started to clear the dishes. Aunt Merry interrupted. "I'll take care of this. Why don't you and your mom go spend some time together? I'm sure there is a lot you need to discuss with the funeral and everything."

Jessi felt herself deflate. She had almost forgotten she was here for her father's funeral. Not that she knew the man. She allowed herself to be led to a sitting room near the front of the house, away from the shouts of laughter and splashing where Mark had taken the kids after supper. No distractions. Jessi looked at her mom. "Why is the funeral so far off? I figured it would be sooner."

"Your father knew many people and had many friends from overseas. It will take those that want to come some time to plan. We thought we'd better hold off for some of his more important clients to get here."

Patty watched her daughter for a moment, trying to decide how much to tell her. There was so much she didn't understand.

Jessi could see the struggle in her mother. She knew she would be having a difficult time if it were Mark's life she was trying to explain. "Mom, you don't have to do this. We don't have to have this chat. It doesn't really matter anyway, does it? I mean, I hardly knew him. It's just a formality. I hardly know either of you. I grew up with my surrogate mother and father, Aunt Merry and Uncle Will. I'm just here because it's the right thing to do."

Patty's hurt mirrored the hurt buried deep in the heart of her daughter. Her grief for her husband was compounded by the hurt she and James had caused their daughter. How she wished she could go back and undo what had been done. But that wasn't possible. The least she owed Jessi was an explanation. No matter how hard it was going to be, she would do it. She would tell her daughter about her and James decisions, the good and the bad. It was time to be up front with her. She only hoped Jessi could somehow forgive her and allow her to be a part of her life. Jessi, Mark, and her grandbabies were all she had left. "No, you have to hear this. You deserve to hear the truth."

Jessi sat down in the over stuffed chair and waited for her mother to bear her soul. She would endure, suffer through the funeral then go home where life would get back to normal. Only then would she retreat back into the safe life she had built for herself.

Patty knew she only had one shot. One chance to get through to the daughter she'd hurt. She had to start at the beginning. It was the only thing she could think of. She stood up, pacing back and forth. "Jessi, all this, all that you see, it didn't used to be this way. Your father has worked very hard to over come his past. He grew up in difficult circumstances. I'm not making excuses for him. I realize that we were wrong, both of us. But, I want you to understand." Her daughter sat motionless. She wasn't going to let this be easy. Patty sat down on the matching ottoman next to her daughter. "Jessi, let me tell you what it was like for your dad growing up. How difficult his home life was. Maybe then you can partly understand his decisions."

Chapter 2
James

James Albert Jackson was born in the middle of a dust storm. He was his parent's first child. They would have seven more before James turned twelve years old. From the population growth within the Jackson household, it was obvious to the outsider that this family was not a part of the ninety percent of Americans that had televisions in their homes. In fact, not only did the Jackson family not have television, but they also had no electricity. Or running water. Or inside plumbing. A person looking in on the Jackson family would think they had traveled back in time to the pioneer days. Such was the life of James Albert Jackson.

It didn't take long for him to figure out his family was different. He went to school. He saw the differences between him and the other kids. He didn't like it. By the time James was fifteen, he had an additional set of twin brothers, bringing the total to an even ten.

He spent his afternoons milking cows and spreading chicken feed, hoping the few chickens they had would lay enough eggs that everyone could have one for breakfast. Rarely did that happen, but he held onto a thread of hope that maybe one day there would be enough food on the table to feed everyone.

They grew or raised most of the food they consumed. And no matter how hard he or his dad worked, there was never enough.

James could never understand why they kept farming. Year after year it seemed the drought or the drop in market values left them near penniless. James decided to leave it all behind the day he turned eighteen. It was a day that sculpted him into the man he was to become. He'd never forget it, not as long as he lived.

James stretched, looking across the room at his brothers. They were still sleeping side by side in the full size bed on the opposite wall. The only reason he had his own was he was too big to squeeze in with the others. He may have only a mattress on the floor, but at least it was his own. Will, his younger brother by ten months was on his own mattress on the floor as well.

He smiled, remembering what day it was. Finally, he was eighteen. *Someone will be fighting for my bed before this day is out.* His own man. He quickly got dressed and made his way downstairs and outside to the barn. Just because it was a day to celebrate didn't stop the chores from needing to be done.

He saw his dad was already working. "Hey pa. Mornin'."

"Mornin'. The stalls need to be mucked out today. You can start that after breakfast."

"Do I have to work on that today? Can it wait til' tomorrow?"

His father looked at him. He didn't take real well to any of his kids talking back. "You'll muck out the stalls like I told you to do. "

James got to work milking the few cows they had. He had nothing to say. What a job for his birthday. He looked around at the muddy ground mixed with cow manure. *What a life. If pa has his way I'll be doing this for the next seventy years of my life. It's bad enough I've done it for the last twelve. Why can't Willy do it? He loves this place, can't pa see that?* The day went from bad to worse.

No one remembered his birthday, not even his mother. He knew not to expect a gift or a cake, but to not even recognize their firstborn's birthday, that was inexcusable, at least in the eyes of an eighteen year old.

By the time he washed up for breakfast there was very little left to eat. His mother was clearing the table. "You must have been dawdling. There ain't much left."

James looked at the pitiful amount of food left. "You expect me to work on an empty stomach? You knew I would be coming in. Why didn't you put something back for me?"

James felt himself being hauled by the back of his shirt and then thrown across the room. "You don't ever speak to your mama that way, you hear me boy? I don't know what's got into you but you better fix it."

James lay in a heap. His head throbbed and his forehead was bleeding. He picked himself up off the floor and went to his room.

After putting everything he owned in one small bag he quietly walked downstairs. His parents were waiting for him.

His dad spoke first. "Where do you think you're going?"

"I'm leaving."

"Oh no you're not."

"Yes, pa, I am."

"You can't. I need you here."

"No, you have Will. He can do everything I was doing. And he wants to. I don't want anything to do with this place."

"This land represents everything for our family. It has been in our family for generations. You can't just turn your back on it. It's your heritage."

"My heritage? You expect me be excited about a falling down decrepit house, a few cows and land we can't even grow cabbage on because it's my heritage? No thanks. You can keep it. I'll make my own heritage."

"There's not too many places a seventeen year old boy can go. I'd think about it before you go heading out."

James looked at his father. "It's a good thing I'm eighteen then, ain't it?" He turned to see if his mother understood. He felt a twinge of remorse as he saw the tears of understanding fill her eyes. He walked over and kissed her cheek. "Bye bye, mama. I'll be seeing you." He walked past Willy, who had heard the whole conversation, and nodded as he left. Even if his father didn't understand it, James had passed the farm to his brother with that single nod. They were close enough that they had always understood one another. Not quite the understanding of twins, but definitely the understanding of two growing boys in a difficult situation.

His father was still yelling as he made his way across the front yard. "You'll come crawling back, I know you will. Just like I did when I was an eighteen year old know it all."

James didn't look back. The sound of his father's voice grew fainter with each step. He could care less about that run down farm and he could care even less what his pa thought. He wouldn't go back to that hellhole if it were the last place on earth to go. He felt a surge of excited anticipation build in the places that before had only felt longing.

He walked for miles. He didn't stop until he stood in front of the recruiting center for the US Army.

* * * *

After basic training, James accepted an invitation to go home with a buddy of his by the name of Fred P. Feldham. James never did learn what that

P. stood for. Fred refused to tell him. Turned out, Fred's family had money. James had his first taste of how the other side lived and he developed a craving for it.

"Fred, you could'a told me you were rich."

Fred looked at his buddy. "Why, would ya not of come?"

James gave this some thought. "Naw, I still would of come but maybe I'd done some shopping first. All I have is my army duds and a couple pair of suspenders. Not the kind of clothes your folks are used to seeing."

"Don't worry about it. We got stores in Houston." Fred grabbed his backpack and headed toward the limousine that sat waiting for them. "We'll have Arthur stop by Sears. They outta have something that'll fit you. And make sure you get some spiffy party clothes. We're going dancin'."

"Dancin'? I don't know how to dance."

Fred laughed. "Don't worry. The girls will be more than willing to teach you."

James practically had his nose pressed against the window, looking at scenery as they made their way through the city. Since he'd joined the army he had more opportunities to see the country and he found he had developed a desire to travel. He wanted to see more.

The limousine pulled up in front of a mansion. James was out of his element. He liked it. Fred's parents met them before they got to the front door. James watched this couple greet their only son. *So this is what caring parents look like.* His parents were as different from Fred's as night was from day. Right off the bat he liked them.

Fred Sr. stepped back and gave James a once over. "So, this is the young man you've been telling me about." He reached for James' hand and gave him a firm handshake. "Welcome to our home. Any friend of Fred's is a friend of ours. Isn't that right, Barbara?"

Barbara took his hand and held it between her two. "That's right. Welcome. Fred Jr. speaks very highly of you. We couldn't wait to meet you. Come on in and get settled. I imagine you're hungry."

James liked the sound of her refined southern drawl. "Thank you for inviting me, Mrs. Feldham, Mr. Feldham. I appreciate your hospitality. Fred has told me so much about the both of you as well. He's a real lucky fella to have you for parents." James grabbed his bags, including the new clothes he had picked up and followed Mrs. Feldham into the large foyer and up the stairs to his bedroom. He'd never seen anything like this.

The days flew by and James found himself spending far more time with Fred Sr. than he did with his army buddy. He was fascinated by the import - export business the man had built for himself. This was the kind of life he wanted. Well, mostly. A nice wife on his arm wouldn't hurt, but he didn't want any kids to tie him down. He wanted success so bad he could taste it.

Half way through the month Fred Jr. insisted he go with him to a concert in Galveston. "Come on. You'll love it. I promise. Besides, there's some girls I want you to meet."

"Ah man, do I have to? I was going to go over some stuff with your dad."

"Yeah, you have to. Besides, dad is the one who got us these tickets. He said you've been working too hard and need to have some fun before we ship out." Fred pulled the tickets out of his pocket. "Elvis is at the Astrodome tonight."

"Elvis?" James had been listening to Elvis since he first came out on the radio every time he had the opportunity. He wouldn't pass this up. "Ah, I need to get cleaned up.

Fred started laughing. "I thought you might change your mind. Besides, we have us a couple of dates. Not that the girls will even look at us during the concert."

James hurried to his room and changed into his best suit. Elvis was someone a man could admire. He came from nothing and made something of himself. He had talent and drive. He had worked hard and made a success of himself. James could learn a lot from a guy like Elvis. He went to comb back his hair and remembered he didn't have much anymore. *So much for being in style.*

James heard the mustang roar to life. He made sure he had some cash in his billfold before he headed downstairs. Wouldn't be right to let Fred pay for their sodas after the concert. He had a date. Even though dating wasn't part of his plan, he was a little nervous about meeting this girl. Her folks were rich too. He wondered if she'd see him for the country hick he was. He hoped not. He was working hard to fit in to this world. Maybe she wouldn't notice.

James took a long look at the Mustang. "Ah man. We're gonna be cramped in that back seat."

Fred just smiled and motioned for him to get in.

The girls came running out of the house as soon as Fred pulled up. The guys got out and Fred introduced both girls to him.

"This is Betty. And this is Patty. Your date."

James took her hand in his and shook it. She giggled. "Nice to meet you, James. You like to be called James? Or Jim?"

"Um, James is fine. You like to be called Patty?"

The petite blond girl nodded.

Fred watched the scene with amusement. "You two gonna stand there all day? We got a concert to get to."

James climbed in the back seat and made room for Patty on the small bench seat. He was sure glad Fred brought this car. He wouldn't have to make an excuse to sit close to her now. Fred turned and looked at him and winked. James had to hand it to him. Fred was pretty smart.

Chapter 3
Jessi

Jessi couldn't contain her excitement. "You mean you and dad's first date was at an Elvis concert?" Even though she was from a younger generation, she had grown up listening to Elvis and had no idea that he played such an important part in her parents' relationship.

"Yep, that is the night I fell in love with your father. He was so unsure of himself. He was lost in a world that was as foreign to him as China would be to you and I. He had no idea how to act or what to say. In fact, we both were a little tongue-tied."

Jessi couldn't believe her ears. "You, tongue tied? That is hard to believe."

"Well, it's true. I was about as unsure of myself as your father was back then. I didn't have much experience in the dating world. My parents were pretty strict and I'd been sheltered. Daddy had different plans for me. He had been grooming a young man to take over his company and take me as his wife. The only problem was, I didn't feel a thing for him. Oh, he was nice enough, but there was no spark."

"Really, you were supposed to marry some other guy?" Jessi was enjoying hearing about her parents past. Even though she had had precious little to do with them as she was growing up, it was still fascinating for her.

"I was. I'll be telling you all about it. Your father played a major role in stopping that wedding."

Aunt Merry chose that moment to enter with the tea tray. "I thought you two could use a little refreshment." She placed the tray of hot tea and cookies on the side table and poured three cups of tea. "Keep on going. I thought I would sit in, if you don't mind. My Will is part of this story."

"Uncle Will and dad are so different. It's hard to believe they come from the same family."

Patty agreed. "Well, events affect each family member differently. Will and James were two very different people." She shook her head. "No, those two were as different as night and day." She wiped her eyes with the tissue tucked in her hand at the reminder that James was no longer with her and smiled at Merry, who had lost Will at a much younger age. She had more time with her husband than many, which was something to be thankful for.

"Your mom is right. Will clung to the family while your daddy ran for all he was worth. He had to make his own way by doing his own thing. He didn't want anything to do with that farm or the land. All he'd ever seen was heartache and hard times, and some dirt wasn't going to make him change his mind." Aunt Merry shook her head. "No, no matter how much his daddy wanted him to take over that farm, he just wouldn't do it."

Patty nodded in agreement. "When your grandpa found out he lost the farm, he blamed your dad. He said if James had stuck around, he wouldn't have lost the farm. Who knows, maybe he was right." Patty took a sip of her tea. "Anyway, back to the story. "The two weeks James had left of his leave was spent between courting me and spending time with Fred's daddy at his business. I don't think your daddy slept much during those two weeks. He used to say. 'I can sleep on the plane'."

Chapter 4
James

James kissed Patty at the plane. He wasn't sure how he'd been talked into letting her see him off. Although, he had to admit to himself it was nice having someone there, someone just for him. He hadn't meant to get attached to anyone.

Patty smiled up at him, a single tear slipping away. She had tried so hard to remain strong. She hadn't known him but a couple of weeks. What would he think? She quickly wiped it away and smiled harder in spite of herself. "You'll be just fine. I know it. And I'll write you. Every day." She wiped another tear away. "You'll be home before you know it."

James pulled the pretty blond into his arms and hugged her close. "I'll write you too." He let her go. He had no experience with women and he had no idea how to make her feel better. He just knew this was something he had to do.

He gripped Mr. Feldham's hand in his own and shook it. His admiration for this man was evident as he said his goodbye. "Thank you for everything. I cannot tell you how much it meant to me that you would involve me in your business dealings while I was here."

Fred Sr. enthusiastically returned the boy's handshake. "It was my pleasure, James. And when you get out, make sure you come see me. I am fairly certain there will be a position here waiting for you."

"Really? I mean, thank you Mr. Feldham. You won't regret it."

"I know I won't son. You be careful over there, do you here?"

"Yes sir, I will."

Fred looked to his son, then back to James. "You two take care of each other, do you hear me?"

Fred Jr. hugged his father. "We will, dad."

"Come home to us, son. Your mother and I will miss you and I fear she'll never recover if anything happens to you."

"Dad, I'll be fine. You'll see. No commie can get the best of a Feldham."

Fred released his father and ran to catch up with James. "Well buddy, looks like it's just you and me now. You ready for this?"

"Yeah, I'm ready. Let's do it."

For all their bravado, neither man had much to say as they made the first leg of the trip. In Alaska when they plane stopped for re-fueling, James watched two soldiers handcuffed together boarding the plane. He nudged Fred and tilted his head. "What's that all about I wonder."

Fred looked to where James was indicating. "Oh, that would be a runner. The coward went awol and now he's being forced to do his duty. We best watch out for him. He probably ain't got what it takes to make it over there. He'll probably freeze up."

There wasn't much talking between the new recruits as they made their way from Alaska to Vietnam. No one knew what to say.

* * * *

The first thing James noticed after his sixteen-hour flight to Vietnam was the beautiful beaches. It was hard to imagine fighting in such a beautiful country. He pulled out the little picture of him and Patty from his pocket. They had ducked into this little photo booth and had a strip of black and whites taken. She took two. He took two. In one she was cross-eyed and he couldn't help but laugh. She would be his good luck charm. A wind came up and the picture went fluttering from his hand. He dove after it then tucked it back in his pocket. *A good luck charm won't offer much good luck if it ain't in my pocket.* He and Fred boarded the bus that was waiting for them.

James tucked himself onto a bench seat and pulled the letter out of his bag. Patty had tucked one into his hand just as he was walking away from Fred and Fred's parents. He had slipped it into his bag and forgot about it. The picture served as his reminder.

My dearest James,

Mama told me to never throw myself at a man or I'd lose his respect. I hope you don't think that is what I am doing. I know I am being forward in writing to you like this and I am being bold, but my heart is telling me what to do and I just can't stop it.

I had the best time with you these past two weeks, more fun than I've had in a long time.

I meant what I said. I'll write to you every day and I'll be praying that you stay safe. I'll be here, waiting for you. If you have time to write me back please do. I will be anxious to know you are safe. If you don't have time, I will understand.

Yours truly,
Patty

James stared hard through the mesh-covered windows of the bus and thought about the short letter Patty sent off with him. He hadn't meant to lead her on and he hoped she would understand when he told her he wasn't ready for a relationship, not yet anyway. There were things he wanted to accomplish first, before getting tied down to a girl. He'd have to write her later and let her down easy. He turned his attention to the new country he was in. Everything was green, everything that is except the brown faces that stoically looked his way as the bus passed. His attention was drawn to the people walking along side the dirt roads they traveled. They seemed almost unaware of the bus and its passengers, their slight glance lacked enthusiasm or interest. He imagined they had seen the same scene so many times over the past few years that this was old hat.

The bus pulled into the base and James grabbed his duffle bag, complete with his fatigues and boots and waited for orders outside his bus. He wouldn't be here long but while he was, he intended to relax and enjoy what was left of the evening. Fred dragged him to the commissary to down a couple of beers and listen to the band mess up their favorite songs. They spent the evening nervously recounting the good times they'd had over the past month.

Fred surprised him when he said he'd proposed to Betty. "I didn't know you were that serious about her?"

"War kinda makes a guy think about the future, you know?"

"Yeah, I know. Thanks for taking me home with you. I really liked working with your dad. That's the kind of stuff I want to do one day."

"He enjoyed having you there. He wants me to take over the family business one day. I guess I'm just used to it so it's not as exciting showing me stuff anymore. Besides, I'll have time for that later."

"Well, all I had growing up was mucking out stalls and milking cows. I would have loved to have your life."

Fred took a drink. "Yeah, I've had a pretty good life."

James nodded his head in agreement.

The next day to James' surprise, both he and Fred were assigned to the same company. They hopped a plane to where the battalion was stationed near Pleiku City. He considered himself lucky. Fred ended up in a different unit and he lost track of him shortly after they got sent out into the boonies. They traveled in small groups making it easier to sneak up on the enemy. Most of the guys in the boonies called them gooks or dinks. It made them less human somehow and easier to shoot them. Day after day James trudged through the forest with a 60lb rucksack on his back. He was a common grunt, low man on the totem pole. Or in Army speak, he had the lowest ranking available and pretty much had to do what he was told. While in Vietnam, a man had plenty of time to think. It was quiet, too quiet. Any noise at all could alert the enemy to their whereabouts and that could mean death for the whole unit. When he was guarding the perimeter, he had to be alert. When his watch was over and if his unit was stationary he would think about life after the war. He often thought of Fred Sr. and the export/import business he wanted so much to be a part of.

Helicopters brought in supplies, including the mail. True to her word, Patty wrote every day. He would receive piles of letters at one time. There wasn't one drop that he didn't receive at least one letter. She even sent the occasional box. The first box contained moldy banana bread. They guys laughed at him. Thankfully she sent cookies after that. The guys didn't laugh when those boxes arrived, they stood in line for a taste of some homemade baking. Even if the cookies were hard, they were a reminder of what was waiting for them at home. James was always willing to share. Some of the guys never received anything from home. James could have been one of those guys if he hadn't of met Patty before leaving stateside.

For some reason, he never wrote her back. He wasn't sure if it was because he wasn't ready to commit to a relationship or if he thought something might happen to him and she'd be spared the pain. Never the less, he never sent one letter in return. He had no problem writing letters to Fred Sr. though. He lived for the days Fred's letters came. The letters coming in from Fred kept him planning for his future. They reminded him of where he was going in life. He didn't allow the letters from Patty to have the same affect on him. He enjoyed hearing about her every day life though. Somehow he could pretend his life was normal.

The jungle caused a man to take stock of his life. It made him consider where he'd been and where he was going. During the quiet times of sitting and waiting, James had nothing but time on his hands. He considered his life up until that point and made decisions based upon his retrospection. Two things he decided upon. He would never be poor again and he did not like anyone telling him what to do. Someday he would be his own boss. During this same time period, he found he was very good at two things, learning languages and selling.

He happened into business in Vietnam quite by accident. Somehow he had been selected to attend a seminar and there he met a guy who knew a guy and before he knew what he got himself into, he was selling some of the rations he has set aside. He never did care for cigarettes, so he had quite a few of those stored up. James also found the more he was around the Vietnamese; the more he understood their language.

It didn't take long and he had his own little business going between the local village Vietnamese and the guys in his unit. He could find anything and make deals that defied logic. One of the locals was always searching him out, trying to sell him useless stuff. Every once in a while the guy would bring him something useful and James would strike a deal with the seller. The locals loved US dollars. Of course, James wasn't supposed to use US money, but he found he could always get a pretty good deal when he used the green stuff and not the play money. If a guy found himself needing something, chances were, James could get it. Soon word had spread and before he knew it, guys outside his unit were seeking him out, trying to find one thing or another. James was more than happy to oblige. He sent the money he made back to Fred Sr. and had him bank it for him. He figured he'd have a little nest egg built up to help him get started when he got back stateside.

The only guy who gave him any grief for selling items at inflated prices was preacher, affectionately called preach by all the guys. Course, the guy wasn't really a preacher, but he carried around his Bible with him like a baby blanket. The guy always had it with him and he was always preaching about forgiveness and salvation. He was a pretty nice fella, even if he did get on a guy's nerves once in a while.

"Hey preach, you need anything? I'm going to the store." That was always how James described meeting up with his middle man.

"Naw, I got everything I need with this." He held up his Bible. "Jimmy, you alright with God? You never know what can happen out here in the jungle." He wiped the sweat from his forehead. It had to be 110 degrees in the shade.

"I got too much luck for anything to happen to me." He pulled out Patty's picture. "See, I've got me a good luck charm here." He showed preach the picture then tucked it back into his pocket where it had been for the last six months.

"There ain't no such thing as luck. You oughta know that."

"Sure there is. Tell you what. You keep God and I'll keep my luck. We'll see which one of us ends up in a better place. How's that sound?"

"Well, if that's the way you want it, I guess I can't do anything about it. I wouldn't put my life in the hands of luck though. It's bad all around. Jesus is the only one I'd trust my life with." With that Preach picked up his Bible and started reading.

James headed to the perimeter where he found his local contact waiting for him. He handed off a carton of cigarettes to the guard on duty and collected a whole satchel of goods then quickly returned to his shelter, which the guys all called a hootch.

He opened the bag and pulled out a small tape player and a few tapes to go with it. The guys would have a bidding war over this thing. There were a few more things in the bag, all stuff he had been looking for. His local contact did good. This would put some money in the bank.

James shouldered the bag and headed out into the night air. He shivered. It would still be considered hot in most parts of the world but compared to the daytime temperatures, it was a bit nippy. Especially once a guy got used to the heat.

He was just about to the hangout when he ran into Preach. "Hey Preach. Where you headed at this hour?"

"Oh, a group of new guys came in and I was chatting it up with them. You know how it goes."

"Yeah, well, I gotta get going." James motioned to the bag hanging on his shoulder.

"You wouldn't happen to have a tape recorder in that bag would you?"

"I just might. Depends on who's asking."

"Well, this new guy was asking about one. Seems he is missing his family pretty bad and has a small fortune to pay for one. You could make a bit of cash if you have one."

"And where might I find this new guy?"

"He's with the lieutenant. I'd make my way toward his hootch and ask around. The guy's name is Will."

James immediately thought of his brother back home. He hadn't given much thought to any of his family since he left. Knowing there was a guy named Will at the camp caused him to reminisce. *Sheesh. Stop it James. There must be a million Wills in the world. Quit actin' all sentimental and get on with it.*

James started toward his lieutenant's tent and watched for the meeting to break up. His higher up knew about his side business but let matters slide as long as James didn't get too greedy with the guys.

The new grunts were a lot safer doing business with him than with some local they didn't know.

A group of grunts walked his way. "Hey, you guys know a Will? I hear he is lookin' for something."

One of the fresh recruits motioned back to the tent. "Yeah, he's just comin' out now."

James nodded. "Thanks." He was almost to the approaching soldier when the full moon came out from behind a cloud. Both soldiers stopped where they were. James was staring straight into the eyes of his brother, Will.

Chapter 5
Jessi

"What?" Jessi looked to her aunt. "You never told me about this."

"I know. There never seemed to be an appropriate time. If I talked about your uncle's time in Vietnam than I would have had to talk about your father's and that wasn't my story to tell."

Jessi turned her head from mother to aunt. "Uncle Will was only 10 months younger than Dad, right? Did he get drafted?"

Aunt Merry nodded her head. "He sure did. And it about killed him. Unlike your father, your uncle loved the farm. He loved everything about it. He knew it would be difficult to be a farmer, but that is all he ever wanted to do. It was too bad your grandfather didn't see that right away. If he had, then his relationship with James would have gone a whole different direction. But, your grandfather was a stubborn man. He couldn't see what was plain in front of him. He only saw what he wanted to see."

Patty joined the conversation. "According to James, Will was really depressed in Vietnam. He ended up giving him that recorder so he could listen to messages from home."

"Yeah, Will told me he sent the money home for his mom to buy a recorder. He lived for those tapes. He always loved being at home. I guess God made everybody to be different."

Jessi nodded her head. "Yeah, I guess so." She tried to stifle the yawn that forced its way out but it had been a long day of traveling.

Patty looked at her watch. "Oh my goodness. I have to meet with the funeral home tomorrow morning. It's already after ten." She glanced at her daughter. "Besides, you're looking pretty tired. Why don't we continue this tomorrow afternoon?"

Aunt Merry stood to collect the tea tray.

"Oh no you don't. I've got that. I'll see you two tomorrow. Goodnight." Patty headed toward the kitchen then watched Jessi and Aunt Merry hug goodnight from the darkened recess of the hallway. Longing filled her but she knew she only had herself to blame. It could have been her Jessi was hugging if only she had chosen her daughter. She had wanted to. God as her witness, she had. But her love for her husband was too great and she didn't want to lose him.

Patty snuggled into her king bed and reached out to feel the empty space next to her. She thought of her daughter downstairs and prayed it wasn't too late for them, for the relationship they could still have. "Please God. Please have mercy on me. Let my little girl come back to me."

She finally fell asleep a few hours before the alarm went off. It would be another long day with another sleepless night to get her through it.

Chapter 6
James

The worst day of the war was the day James got the news that Fred Jr. had been killed in action. He dreaded not being there to comfort Fred's parents when they got the news. It was rotten luck really. They had three weeks left till they shipped out and Fred had to go and get himself killed. A sniper took him out. He had sneezed and the shot rang out seconds later. Fred didn't have a chance.

Preach tried to console James with his talk of heaven and salvation, something about Fred accepting Jesus so he was in a better place now. James wanted nothing to do with such talk.

"Preach, you can keep your thoughts to yourself on this one. I don't want to hear it."

James served his last three weeks and managed to see Will before he left. "You stay alert you hear me? And don't do anything stupid. You wait till you get to camp before you start listening to them tapes of yours. Get home safe. Ma needs you."

Will hugged his brother then released him. It was going to be a lonely place without James. "I'll do my best. I've got God. He'll protect me."

* * * *

James stepped off the plane and instinctively knew the waiting limousine was for him. He approached the vehicle with a surety that he lacked the first time he road in the luxury car. Fred Sr. met him at the door and shook his hand then pulled him into a fatherly embrace. "Good to have you home, son."

"It's good to be back, sir."

James stepped into the shoes that had been left vacant and no one ever questioned his place in the family. Sometimes he caught Fred Jr's mother gazing into the distance. He knew she missed her son. But he could do nothing to change the situation so he never addressed the pain he knew she felt. The first day he had arrived he had told her how sorry he was and she had cried on his shoulder, holding him like she would have liked to hold her son. Since that wasn't possible, she held onto the boy in his place with all her strength. Never again did they speak of his friend's death.

He was offered a suite of rooms so he had his privacy yet was within the walls that housed and shielded the Feldham family from the prying eyes of the public. He was one of theirs now and they would do whatever necessary to keep him safe.

James fell into the family business like he was, well, family, which is exactly how everyone viewed him. From the servants to his fellow employees, everyone knew who he was and what his position was from the start, heir to the throne. No one questioned it. No one confronted and no one complained. To do so would be to lose whatever position they currently held and besides, no one worked harder than James. It didn't take long before secret grudges turned into open admiration. He was impressive. His natural knack for sales and the languages he picked up while in Nam gave him an edge in the area of foreign exports and imports. James made a whole lot of money for the Feldham Corporation.

By Christmas of his first full year of being home, when the bonuses were handed out, not a single employee had any doubt whatsoever that James was the sole cause for the checks being the largest they had ever seen.

It was on an uncustomary stop by the Houston Galleria to pick out gifts for Fred Sr. and his wife, Barbara, that he ran into Patty. Up to this point, James had not made public appearances nor had he attended any of the social functions that the Feldham family was often invited to, so he hadn't had the opportunity to see the girl who had written him 365 letters, just like she'd promised.

James had the good sense to blush when he saw her and said the first thing that came to mind. "I got your letters, all 365 of em'."

Patty went white. She had given up on James. When she had made the promise to write him, it was under the wrong assumption that the attraction she had felt was mutual. He looked taller, if that were possible. And more handsome. She squared her shoulders and tilted her chin slightly upward. "I'm glad you made it home safe. If my letters helped in anyway, then it was worth it." She nodded goodbye and started toward the next store, glancing quickly at the diamond engagement ring on her finger.

James stood in stunned silence as he watched her walk away. He wasn't sure what happened, but before his brain could catch up with his heart he took off at a jog after her. "Hey, Patty. Wait up."

She turned and felt her heart drop. She still loved this man, she only wished he loved her too.

He quickly reached her side. "Do you want to get a cup of coffee and catch up?"

She hesitated and twirled the ring on her finger. "I'm not sure that would be appropriate, seeing as I'm engaged and all."

James eyes instantly reached the diamond solitaire on her ring finger. "Well, I see you've made some lucky guy happy. But, can't we have a coffee? We're still friends, right?"

"I guess a cup of coffee can't hurt. There's a little café down the street."

James led her outside to his car. "I can bring you back here after. No sense in both of us driving." He opened the passenger side door for her.

"Thank you." Patty remained quiet on the short drive. She would let him lead the conversation and she promised herself she wouldn't have any female hysterics over this lost love.

James pulled into the café and jumped out to open her door.

He ordered coffee and pie for both of them. At first the conversation was strained, neither one knew quite what to say. James decided he had to apologize and explain things to her. It was only fair.

"I'm sorry I never wrote you back. I read every letter. Sometimes over and over again. Then I'd get a whole batch of them at one time and line them up in order by their postmark. I'd open one at a time. I loved hearing about your life here at home. At first I didn't want to write you because I wasn't sure I was ready for a relationship and I wasn't sure any woman would want me after she found out that I don't want kids." And then, later, I didn't know what to write about." He sipped his coffee. "War was terrible. The jungle was terrible. The heat was terrible. I just didn't want to talk about it."

She reached out and covered his hand with hers. "I'm sorry too." She looked out the window before she continued. "At first, I told myself it would take months to get your letters. Then, when Betty started sharing parts of Fred's letters, I imagined you in the heart of the jungle, with nothing to write. I guess I made things up to keep from being hurt and looking the fool in front of my friends."

"No, it's all my fault. I should have been more considerate. I can't imagine how you felt. I just wanted to say I'm sorry." James drained the last of his coffee and stood up. He still felt as clumsy around this girl as a newborn calf fresh from her mama. He was thankful his behavior didn't carry over to his business relationships. If they had, he'd have no choice but to head back to the farm.

James told Patty goodbye and wished her well and much happiness for her upcoming wedding as he dropped her off at her car.

He headed home with his purchases, a brooch for Barbara and a diamond studded cigarette case for Fred Sr. He'd had them gift wrapped, so he could place them discreetly under the tree and none would be the wiser. He tried to keep his thoughts from returning to his conversation with Patty. Easier said than done. When they'd been apart it had been easy to shift her to the back burner. Now that he'd seen her, it was proving a little more difficult. She'd gotten under his skin the first time and he chalked it up to everything new happening to him. This time, he was a seasoned traveler, a rising star in the business world and running in social and financial circles he had never known to exist and she still had the same affect on him. He was in trouble.

Christmas passed quietly in the Feldham household. Even though words were kept to a minimum concerning Fred Jr's passing, Christmas was especially hard. The family celebrated Christmas Eve then sent the staff home to be with their families. After everything was cleaned up, Fred, Barbara and James settled in the living room. James had never seen such a tree in all of his life. It was at least fifteen feet tall and nearly reached the ceiling. There were enough white lights on the upright structure to almost light up the room. There were too many ornaments to begin to count. Barbara said they were family heirlooms, collected over the years from generation to generation.

James thought about the Christmas tree in his family home. His mama had saved all year so she could buy one of those silver artificial trees that had become popular. It wasn't very big, but she was sure proud of it. He wondered what she would think of this tree. The Feldhams had it cut down way up north and had it flown in special. She would probably faint at how much it cost.

He savored the taste of nutmeg as he drank his eggnog. He had learned to take every new experience in stride, making sure he was comfortable in his new role as a rich man living in a rich man's world. He set his glass on the coaster and retrieved his gifts from under the tree. Both Feldhams loved the gifts he'd purchased and seemed to appreciate the fact that he had done so personally. In return, they lavishly presented him with an appointment with Fred Sr.'s personal tailor to have a new wardrobe made. Fred Sr. stood and handed him an envelope that awarded him ten percent ownership in the company.

"You have made all the difference this year in the company's growth. We thought this was an appropriate thank you." Fred returned to his place next to his wife, took her hand and stared at the tree.

James wished them both a Merry Christmas then excused himself to his rooms. He took the document out of the envelope and ran his fingers over the print. The accountants would explain everything to him first thing Monday morning, but if he were to guess, his income level just increased dramatically. He smiled to himself before his mind wandered to a certain blond who had invaded his thoughts and his senses. How was he going to get this woman out of his system? Every woman wants children and he made the decision a long time ago that children were not part of his future. How could he ask this of a woman? No, he had to let her go. She would be better off with this guy she was marrying. They'd have a bunch of kids and she'd be happy. With James, that wouldn't happen. He turned off the light on the end table and tried to close his mind off when he closed his eyes. It didn't work.

James drifted from thought to thought. He wondered if his brother had made it home okay and he wondered if the family was having a nice Christmas. He'd love to be a fly on the wall tomorrow when Santa showed up. The kids would freak. The thought made him smile. His father would know where the gifts came from. Hopefully he accepted them and let the kids have the few toys he sent. It was the least he could do. He might not want to spend the rest of his life toiling in the dirt and the sun, but he could do a little something for his younger brothers and sisters now and again. And for his mama. She'd always complained about having cold hands in the winter. He'd sent her some special hand lotion to help her dry and bleeding skin as well as some soft suede gloves lined with rabbit fur. He was sure she had never owned something so nice. Maybe once they got their gifts, they would understand what was available on the other side of the farm. Maybe his father would finally get why James didn't want to follow in his father's footsteps.

His mind drifted from one thing to another, finally settling on Patty. She was getting married on New Years Day. Did he want to let her go? Would she have him if he gave her the choice?

He could support a wife now. He knew that. Did she understand he really didn't want kids? He pushed back the covers and got to his feet and stood before the tall window at the far end of his living quarters. He had a clear view of the city. He loved this city. Vibrant. Alive. With every step he took, with every deal he made he could feel her pulse. Houston had become as much a part of him as the breath that gave him life. Did Patty have a part in that life as well?

Monday, back at the office, confirmed what he had already suspected, he was a rich man. Now if he could just keep Patty from occupying his every thought.

The day of her wedding quickly approached. She was marrying at sunset and he was invited, along with Fred Sr. and Barbara. James noticed Betty, Fred's former fiancée, was Patty's maid of honor. That had to be hard on her after losing Fred in the war.

Every one stood, the bride must be approaching. James craned his neck to get a look at her. Wow. He almost whistled out loud then remembered where he was and who he was. He no longer allowed himself to participate in crass behavior.

She was an angel in a long white gown and she smiled radiantly. Obviously she was happy. Then he caught her gaze and for a split second he saw hesitation in her. She would choose him. If he had given her the choice, she would have chosen him. He watched her, on the arm of her father, slowly approach the altar and the man who had won her. She had pearls wound up in her hair. Had he ever noticed a detail like that before? He wanted to reach out and pull her to him. She was his. Or she should be. He loved her. Why was he just realizing that now? When it was too late?

He heard the words of the priest. He heard the exchanging of the vows. He watched them light the candles. He saw them place the rings on the fingers. Then he heard the priest utter the final words before he announced them as man and wife. "If any of you has reasons why these two should not be married, speak now or forever hold your peace."

For a split second there was silence then he looked into her eyes and his heart won. "Yes, because I love her."

The church was a collective gasp and every eye turned to him. He made his way to the center aisle and approached the bride, speaking as he walked. "I love you, Patty. I know this is not the most opportune time to tell you, but I had to say it. I had to give us a chance. I can't stop thinking about you. And I think you love me too."

Her hand was covering her mouth and tears were streaming down her cheeks. He didn't know whether she was happy or angry with him for interrupting the wedding. He knew he'd have to answer for his behavior later, but he'd deal with it. He'd learned in Vietnam that once in a while, you had to go for it and suffer the consequences. This was clearly one of those times. If she refused him, he'd be the laughing stock of the city. But if she accepted, forgiveness would be quick in coming.

He lifted his hand in quiet pleading, begging her to accept his invitation.

Chapter 7
Jessi

Jessi almost choked on her sweet tea. "You have to be kidding me. He did not do that!" She had hung out all morning with Mark and the kids by the pool. Secretly, she couldn't wait for her mother to return so she could hear more of her parents' story. Somehow the words were filling a part of her long left empty.

Patti raised her eyebrows and returned her daughter's gaze. "Oh yes he did."

"Well? What did you do?"

"What do you think I did? Isn't it obvious?"

"You took his hand? Right there in the sanctuary in front of all those people?"

"I did. And my intended punched your father so hard he laid him out flat. I can't say he didn't deserve it. He could have called me before the wedding. That was your father though; he didn't rush any decision until he absolutely had to. It was good for his business. Not so good for his private life."

"Wow. You guys led some kind of crazy life. I mean, who does that kind of thing? Did you get married right away?" Jessi took a bite of her salad.

"It wasn't long after that. Of course your father wanted to get some things settled before he took a wife. He bought a house. Not near as grand as the one he was living in, but it was a beautiful house nonetheless. And then after the large fiasco from the almost first wedding, we decided to marry quietly on the beach while the sun was setting over the city then have a quiet supper with the Feldhams and my parents. In so many ways, it was much better. At least I was marrying the man I loved with all my heart. I knew the first time I laid eyes on him, that he was the one."

"So, the dress I got married in was from you and daddy, right?"

"Yes, that was the very same dress. And it looked beautiful on you too. I'm so glad you agreed to wear it." Patty wiped a tear from her eye at the memory of seeing her daughter marry in the beautiful ivory dress. Of course had Jessi and Merry been near to the same body size and shape, Jessi would rather have worn her aunt's dress. Still, it gave Patty some satisfaction to know her daughter took a small part of her mother to her wedding day.

Patti continued. "James did not let anyone from his family know that he was getting married. He kept it quiet for several years. When he received an invitation to his brother Will's wedding was when they found out about me. It was also the first time since his 18th birthday that he'd stood face to face with his father.

Aunt Merry entered the conversation. "This is where I come in." She washed down the crumbs from her blueberry crumb cake with her tea. "You already know most of my story, but you don't know about your uncle and everything he endured. She scooted back on the love seat and settled in. "Your uncle was lost when your father was discharged from Vietnam."

Chapter 8
Will

Will had never felt so completely alone. He missed his family. He missed the farm. He missed the animals. He never adapted to Vietnam, not even in survival mode. He wanted out. He wanted to go home.

One day walking through the jungle, a buddy of his tripped a land mine and Will took a hit of shrapnel in the leg. The field doctors weren't sure if he would lose his leg and they shipped him stateside for surgery. He never regained use of his leg and he never returned to Vietnam. He got his wish, but he never figured he'd go home less of a man. If his chances of inheriting the farm were slim before, they were impossible now. He'd be a cripple the rest of his life and his father would never accept that.

When he returned home, he got a small first floor apartment and got a job working at the post office. He couldn't deliver the mail, but he could stand at the window good as anybody. And, he started attending The Gospel Church, where he met the love of his life, Merry.

She was pretty as anything. Hurt too, he could tell. When he found out she wouldn't be able to have children of her own, and she tried to tell him she wasn't good enough for him, well that did him in. He knew God put her in his life and he knew this was the woman he was supposed to spend the rest of his days with. God would take care of the children. He always had a plan. Even if Will couldn't understand how, God always had his back. Yeah, he was plenty sore about his leg, but his buddy lost his life. So, he had an awful lot to be thankful for too.

After six months of courting, he asked Merry to be his wife. She made him the happiest man alive when she said yes. He placed the small diamond ring on her finger but he had one request before they married, and that was to invite his brother for the wedding. He wanted his older brother to stand up for him. The trick was, he had to find him first. Then he had to get him to say yes. Finding him would be the easy part.

Will had enough information about James' friend Fred to know the general vicinity James lived in. Combined with his recourses at the post office, he found his address and sent him a letter, literally begging him to not only attend the wedding, but to be his best man.

There was nothing Will could do but wait. It was in God's hands.

Chapter 9
James

James re-read the letter for the third time and ran his hands through his hair. Go back home to face his father? He held his breath for a quick second and let it go. How could he? Yet, it was Will asking so how could he not? He was caught between his own fear of facing his father and his self-imposed status of protector of his younger brothers and sisters. Even if said younger brother was almost as old as he was.

Regardless of the decisions he had to make, the content of the letter made James smile. His younger brother found the woman of his dreams. He could picture the future with a bunch of little Will's running around. Will always wanted a big family. Now he was starting it. He had to be happy.

How could he not go? He could handle his father. He looked around his office, at the rich cherry furniture, at the view of the city from his 10th floor office windows. He was somebody. This might be the perfect time to return home, to show his father he'd become somebody, in spite of that good for nothing farm. His father was the one who said he'd never become anything.

He slipped the letter into his pocket, told his secretary he was leaving early and headed home to his wife, Patty to tell her they were headed to Oklahoma.

The wedding took place in spring in the small church where Will and Merry met. It was a simple affair, in some ways more so than James' own wedding, although there were certainly more in attendance. He chuckled. That wasn't hard to accomplish. The number of siblings alone out numbered those who attended James' wedding.

James stood at the front of the church with his brother while he waited for his bride, Merry. He watched his brother's face as she approached the altar. Will had always been an open book and did not disappoint those who knew him well. He was in love. Smitten. A goner. There just weren't words to describe the joy on his brother's face. James wondered if he'd radiated the same look of love on his wedding day. Did his eyes betray his heart in the same manner? Some how he doubted it. He had never been able to open himself up the same way Will was able to.

He looked at his father who still refused to look at him. So much for letting bygones be bygones. Of course there was none better at holding a grudge than his father.

The ladies of the church put on the reception and the selection of food was as eclectic as the attendees with James and Patty in their finery and a few cousins running around barefoot and in bibs. It sure was interesting. James watched his wife, certain that she was being entertained.

Before eating, James introduced Patty to his mother. "Mama, this is Patty, my wife."

Patty extended her hand. "Mrs. Jackson, it's so good to finally meet you."

James' mother turned to see where her husband was. As far as he was concerned, she was fraternizing with the enemy.

James understood her dilemma. He kissed her check then guided his wife to the food line and to the table that they were sharing with Will and Merry. He enjoyed spending time with his brother and sister in law. He would be equally glad when it was time to go home.

Will and Merry were already seated at the little table reserved for the four of them by the time James and Patty arrived with their full plates.

James pulled out Patty's chair and joked with his brother. "I see you managed to get all these ladies to make your favorite foods. You must have them wrapped around your little finger."

"Yeah, they love me. What can I say?" Both brothers and their wives laughed, but all four knew the statement was pure truth. There was something about Will that brought out the best in people. James commanded respect and awe; Will was loved by all. James was okay with the arrangement. He wasn't looking for love. He was looking for success. And by all accounts he had found it.

James groaned as he chewed the sweet cornbread in his mouth. The only thing he missed besides his mama and his siblings, from living at the farm, was the taste of good southern cooking. "So, when are you two planning on starting a family?"

Will looked at his bride, hoping she would remain strong. "Well, we'll see what family the Lord provides us with. All in God's timing, right honey?" He squeezed Merry's hand.

She smiled at her husband. She had come to terms with their situation and trusted God implicitly when it came to having a family. She still felt guilty about not being able to give Will the children she knew he wanted. But when she had told him she couldn't have children and tried to end the relationship, he put his foot down and told her she was the woman God had set aside for him. He believed God would provide a family for them. Somehow Will's strong belief that God would bring them a child gave her the courage to believe as well. Not that she was ready to tell her story to her new brother in law and his wife. She would have to get to know them better before that happened. Merry squeezed her husband's hand in return, thankful for his strength. He had given her hope where there hadn't been much previously. "That's right. We're trusting the Lord. He'll give us children as He sees fit."

James wrapped his arm around his wife as he and all the other guests wished the best for the happy couple as they left for their honeymoon. James had tucked a little extra cash in his brother's hand before Will left. He knew money was tight and wanted his brother to enjoy his few days away.

He looked toward his father who was still keeping his distance. It was now or never. He closed the gap that had separated them the entire day. "Hey, pops. Nice wedding huh?"

His father grunted in response.

"Seems like Will met a real nice girl."

"It would seem."

"Pops, you gonna stay mad at me forever?"

"You got that right, boy. You're the reason we're losing the farm. You're the reason your mama has to leave the only real home she ever had. You think I'm gonna forgive you for doing that?"

"What are you talking about?"

"The bank is taking the farm back boy. If you had done your job by us as you should have, this wouldn't be happening. Now we're losing the farm. Been in our family for generations. Losing it all cause our son is too high and mighty to be a farmer. I hope you are proud of yourself. Coming up here all dressed up like some rich man, showing off to your kin. You see what you've gone and done? Forgive you? I don't think so."

"Wait just a minute, pops. I was never cut out for farming and you know it. Every idea I had to make that place earn its keep you shot down. You wouldn't try a thing I suggested. And now you blame me cause your losing the place? Ain't that..." James closed his eyes and corrected himself. "Isn't that a case of the pot calling the kettle black? You say you wanted my help but you wouldn't listen to a word I had to say. What you wanted was someone to clean out your stalls and do your bidding at every turn. You didn't want the farm to run better or more efficient. You wanted it to run like it always had. Well, you got your wish. Only this time, the government didn't bail you out. You lost the farm. Not me."

James watched his father's face grow red then watched him drop to his knees. "Somebody, call for help. Dad is having a heart attack." He fell to the floor next to his father and saw hatred spilling from his pain filled eyes and heard one accusing word come from the trembling lips. "You..." Then his father went still in his arms.

He watched as the second long black car left the church. The first to leave was filled with promise and new life, the second was filled with death and pain. James would always remember this day, the day he sent his father to meet his maker.

Chapter 10
Jessi

Jessi looked around the eerily silent room. "So, daddy died the same way as his daddy."

Both Patty and Merry were staring into their teacups remembering that day like it was yesterday.

Patty closed her eyes while her memories rushed forward "Your father felt so guilty. He became a different man after that. He had always been driven, always had goals, but things changed. He became so focused, so intent on becoming successful that he let everything else in his life blur."

She stood up, needing to exert some energy. "He bought a nice house in town for your grandma and made sure she and his younger siblings always had what they needed. He did not neglect his duties. But he never again revealed his heart. He closed up tighter than a drum." She turned and faced her daughter. "Even to me."

Merry set her cup on the side table. "I remember being so happy. Finally, I was the blushing bride and I was ready to spend my first night with your Uncle Will. We talked about our dreams the entire ride to the resort. We didn't waste a moment. It was a good thing too. As soon as we climbed out of the limo, a resort messenger was waiting for us, bad news in hand. We were devastated. Will, because his father had passed. Me, I'm embarrassed to admit, because my long weekend with my husband was shattered. I had so looked forward to that time away. I was heartbroken. We spent the four-hour ride home in silence. I wish I had been more of a comfort to him, but I was acting selfishly and pouting."

Jessi put her hand on her Aunt's knee. "Of course you were devastated. Who wouldn't be?"

Merry blinked away the tears. "I should have been there for my husband. He was crushed. All along he had wanted his father's approval. He wouldn't let jealousy come between him and James, but his father didn't make it easy. James was the golden boy in their father's eyes and Will's war injury only reinforced his father's opinion of him. He was told in no uncertain terms that the family farm would not be his, especially when he came home a cripple. He never got the opportunity to prove his father wrong, that he could make the farm a success. He never received the blessing that every father should bestow upon his children. Even though he never complained, I could tell through the years the hurts were still there buried deep."

Chapter 11
Will

Will wiped the tears from his own eyes before wiping his wife's. "Honey, we knew this could happen."

Every month became a cycle. Merry anxiously waiting to see if this would be the miracle month and she would become pregnant. She just knew that God was going to provide her and Will a baby of their own to love. Each month brought the same heartache and for days afterward she would cry on Will's shoulder and ask God why?

"Would you like to go and see a doctor?" He'd been thinking about it for months and didn't want to get her hopes up, but he just didn't know any other way to get her to let it go and let God work his miracle in his timing, not hers. Maybe a doctor would either know how to fix their problem, or tell them in no uncertain terms they just couldn't have a baby. Maybe then she'd listen to reason. It made him regret ever bringing up the possibility of a miracle.

Merry sniffled, wiping her nose with his handkerchief. "Could we? Really?" She threw her arms around her husband. She had always known that it would take a miracle for her to have a child. She felt hope like she hadn't in so long. "God can perform miracles through doctors, isn't that right Will?"

He wrapped her in his arms. "Yes, honey. God can work miracles any way he sees fit."

The following Monday morning Will and Merry found themselves seated in their small town doctor's office.

Most small towns are quite aware of everyone else's business; this small town was no exception. Seeing as how these three attended the same church together and how often Will and Merry were the object of much prayer concerning their situation, Doc was very familiar with their problem. "Will, Merry, you both know how much I have been praying for you. I'm glad you finally came to see me. Sometimes God chooses to speak a miracle into existence and sometimes he works miracles through people, like doctors." He closed the chart he was holding and set it on his desk. "This goes beyond my scope of expertise, but I have a friend in Houston who is a specialist in fertility. If you can work it out, I'd like you to go and see him."

Will turned to Merry, eyebrows raised. " We could stay with James and Patty. I'm sure they would have us. And I have vacation time coming at the post office. What do you think?"

Merry's smile said everything that needed saying.

"Well, Doc. We'd like for you to make that phone call."

"Consider it done. I'll give you a call when I get things set up."

Will shook doc's hand and Merry hugged him goodbye. "Thanks, Doc. It really means a lot."

The two left the office feeling lighter than they had in some time. Maybe now, he'd get his wife back. "You feel like getting some lunch? I have the rest of the day off."

Merry entwined her arm with his and tilted her head. "Yeah, let's walk. I just can't help but think God is going to give us our miracle, Will. I just know He is."

"Me too, Merry. Me too."

Chapter 12
James

Patty counted down the days on the calendar. She was late. Her chin dropped and she closed her eyes. What was she going to do? James was going to go crazy when he got home from his trip to China. He was still going to be gone another two weeks. Maybe she was just late. Problem was, she was never late. Rain, snow, sleet or hail, she was always on time. If she didn't start her cycle in the next week, she'd make a doctor's appointment. She pasted on a smile and cast her worry aside. She had stayed home from this trip for a reason, she had things to do and she wasn't going to let this keep her down. She tied her light blue chiffon scarf around her newly put up hair and made her way outside and into her brand new convertible. The city was waiting and one must not keep the city waiting.

The week passed in a whirlwind of girlfriend lunches and bridge. While she missed James when she chose to stay home, she enjoyed the freedom it gave her to catch up with friends. She was expected to play the perfect hostess to James' business associates and that required much of her time, as he often entertained at home for those he wished to do business with. Financially, their life was a raging success. And their relationship had its good points too. Even though James had closed himself up emotionally, he was still a good man, thoughtful, caring and generous to a fault. She smiled as she ran her hand over her brand new car. Yes, he was more than generous. She remembered where this beautiful car was taking her and she quickly replaced the smile with a grim expression. "Please God, don't let me be pregnant." She wasn't much for praying, but this seemed like a very good time to start.

An hour later, the doctor confirmed what she already knew. She was pregnant. She left in tears, wondering what she was going to tell her husband. Abortion was out. She knew women had them freely nowadays, but she just couldn't. She was having a baby. As scared as she was, she was going to go through with this pregnancy. This would be the one thing she would make sure she got her way on. James would not take this baby away from her. He would not do it. She had three days till he got home to come up with her case. She just had to convince him.

* * * *

Three days had passed and Patty was no closer to a resolution than she had been the day she found out, or for that matter, the day she suspected she might be pregnant. Now James was due home any minute. She would have to find the perfect time to tell him. Despite her anxiety over telling her husband, she found herself smiling, thinking about the little life that was growing inside her. Knowing James didn't want any children and agreeing to marry him anyway, she had known there was little hope that she would ever have the satisfaction of having a child.

For four years she had been so careful. Every once in a while she would bring up the possibility but he refused to even talk about it, and he would always remind her she agreed before they got married. She couldn't deny that she did indeed agree. But her desire to have a baby never lessened. The sound of a car door demanded her attention.

James seemed full of energy when he arrived home and insisted they go out to eat at one of his favorite restaurants, a high-end restaurant where they were sure to see some of his clients. It was going to be a long evening.

The maitre d' seated them at their favorite table. After placing their napkins on their laps, Patty began to fidget. She knew she had to tell him, but this was definitely not the place. Even though his reaction would be controlled, he would see it as manipulation. No, it would be much better to tell him in the privacy of their home.

James took a sip of his wine. "You're awfully quiet this evening."

"I'm sorry. It's been a long day. Why don't you tell me about your trip?"

James spent the better part of the next hour talking about his buying trip. He met up with several of his more important clients in Asia as well as a few potential clients. He deemed the trip a success. He looked at her barely touched salmon. "Are you sure you're not coming down with something? You hardly touched your food."

Fear ripped through her. Had he figured it out? "Really, I'm just tired. You know how I catch up with all my friends when you're away. It wore me out this time. I guess I get more rest when I'm on the road with you."

Though not convinced, James nodded anyway. "Okay, well, you'd know if you were getting sick. I worry about you. Next time, you're coming with me. Then I can keep an eye on you."

She could just imagine him toting around a pregnant wife, introducing her to his clients. He would just love that. No, she wouldn't be going with him next time but this was not the time to argue about it. "When are you going back?"

"I'm probably going back to China next spring. But, in August I'm heading to Germany, Austria and Poland. You haven't been on that trip. We'll take a few days to see the sights. It'll be fun."

She really didn't have the energy to think about traipsing through Europe. What she really wanted to do was pick out nursery furniture and a layette. Her emotions started taking over and she quickly excused herself and made her way to the ladies room.

Get a grip Patty. He already knows something is up. You start crying all over the place and he'll know before you have a chance to tell him.

She splashed some cool water onto her face and returned to the table with her smile in place.

James watched his wife as she made her way to their table. Something was wrong. He was perceptive, in his line of work he had to be. And he knew when his wife was out of sorts. "I think you need to see the doctor. Let's make an appointment tomorrow."

His words sunk in as she pulled out her chair to sit. So, there would be no putting this off. He would have to be told tonight. "Let's see how I feel in the morning, okay?"

He motioned for their waiter then waited for the driver to pull up with the car. He opened the door for her then went around and let himself in. "I'm tucking you into bed as soon as we get home."

Patty laid her head against the back of the seat and closed her eyes. *God, please help him understand.*

Upon arriving, instead of climbing the stairs to the bedroom, she turned to her husband, begging him to understand with her eyes.

"Patty, what is it? What is wrong?"

"Can we sit down? I need to talk to you."

"Of course." He led her to the davenport and sat down next to her.

After taking a deep breath, she just came out with it. "James, I'm pregnant." His face was void of all emotion. Nothing. He didn't say a word, he just stared at her. "James, please, say something."

James watched his wife, tears streaming down her face. Not even her tears could sway him. She had never used tears before to get what she wanted. She had never needed to use theatrics. Now, the tears were flowing like a faucet. "Why did you do this?"

"I didn't do this. We did this."

"You know what I mean. You let this happen. I told you I didn't want kids."

"I didn't do it on purpose, at least give me a little bit of credit."

He stood up and paced back and forth in front of the fireplace. He turned to face her. "This ruins everything, Patty. Everything. I have worked and worked to make a better life for us. A child requires constant attention. Everything in our lives will have to revolve around this baby." He ran his hand through his hair. "How am I supposed to do that when I am on the road half the year? Can you tell me that?"

"You won't have to. I'll take care of her."

"Her? You already know it's a her?"

"James, please. I want this baby."

"What happened to the life we planned? Working hard in the beginning and the traveling around the world as we got older? What happened to that? All our hopes and dreams have been erased in a single careless moment."

"No, James. You might not have wanted children but I have always wanted them. I gave in to your selfishness because I love you. Those are your dreams. Not mine. Everything that matters to me is right here. You, me, and this baby. That's what my dreams are made of."

What could he say? It was a done deal. She would have to handle everything from doctors' appointments to the delivery. He could make no guarantees. "Fine, have it your way. But, this is all on you. I make no promises."

She ran to him and threw her arms around his neck. "Thank you. I promise, I'll take care of her. You won't have to worry about a thing."

Chapter 13
Will

The back door slammed, letting Merry know Will was home. She yelled out. "Doc called and everything's set for next month. We just need to call James and see if we can stay with them."

Will followed the sound of his wife's voice and found her standing in front of the mirror, brushing her hair. He put his arms around her and snuggled in. "Mmm, you smell good. You look pretty too. Are we going somewhere?"

"No, can't a woman look good for her husband just because she wants to?"

"Hearing from Doc didn't do anything to help your mood along did it?"

"Well, maybe a little." She turned to face him. "Can you call James? Will, I'm just so excited. I just know this is God's plan."

"Of course. I'll go call him now." Will headed toward the kitchen. "Babe, smells like something is burning in here."

"Oh no. I forgot about the roast." Merry started clearing the smoke with her hand. She choked she opened the oven door. "I think it's ruined. I'm so sorry. Can we have grilled cheese again?"

"How about we celebrate tonight instead. You look too pretty for grilled cheese." He stretched the phone to the kitchen table and dialed. "Let me confirm with James that we are welcome then we'll drive into the city. How does that sound?"

"I'm ready as soon as you are."

The phone rang several times before Will heard a voice at the other end. "Patty? Hi, it's Will. Is James there? Can I speak with him?"

Will had to wait for a moment before hearing the sound of his brother's voice. He spent the next ten minutes telling James what was happening in their life and after being assured they were most welcome and giving him the dates, he hung up and got ready for his date. He too felt God was going to work a miracle and give them the baby they desired. He just wasn't sure how God planned on doing it.

Chapter 14
Jessi

"So, mom, you were pregnant and didn't want to be and Aunt Merry, you wanted to be pregnant and weren't. That had to go over well."

Patty kicked off her shoes and propped up her feet. "You have to remember. Neither one of us knew each other's secrets. We were both too ashamed, for obvious reasons."

Merry chimed in. "I was so ashamed of what I had done when I was a young girl, I didn't tell anyone but Will. It wasn't until much later, after some growing up in God, that I realized we all sin, in fact none of us are without sin, and He is fully able to forgive us and forget our sins as far as the east is from the west."

Jessi thought long and hard. "Mom, did daddy want you to abort me?"

"I can honestly say your father never once asked me to abort you. I truly thought he would, and I was prepared to fight him on it, but he never did." She propped a pillow behind her back. "I waited for him to bring it up but as the days passed, I realized that was not his intention. Your father was always one to face his responsibilities and you were no exception. Through out the years he made sure you always had what you needed. Even though he never responded to you emotionally, physically you were always provided for through the work of his hand."

"It sure would have been nice to have felt his love just once. I always felt like I was in his way, like I was a bother."

Patty didn't know what to say. It was true. He did make her feel that way, not because he said those things, but because of what he never said.

Jessi racked her brain trying to remember if she ever heard the words 'I love you' from her father. "Mom, do you ever remember dad telling me he loved me? I don't recall a single time."

Patty smiled. "I think we're getting ahead of ourselves a little bit. I promise, before all this is through, you'll know your father loved you beyond a shadow of a doubt. I know it, Jessi. You have a great capacity to forgive. It's in your makeup, especially when you know all the circumstances." Patty stood up. "I'm going to take a potty break then make us some sandwiches. I'm getting hungry. I hope Mark and the kids are having fun at Frontier City."

After a quick phone call to check on her family, Jessi settled at the kitchen table with her mom and aunt. "So, aunt Merry. What I really want to know is when did you learn how to cook?" All three women started laughing.

Merry didn't feel that question justified an answer. "Everyone ready to go on?"

Patty addressed Merry. "Yes, we can eat as we talk. Let's tell Jessi how much she was loved, shall we?"

Chapter 15
Will

Merry stood on the front step of James and Patty's house and was speechless. She knew her brother and sister-n-law had money, but she had no idea they lived like this. "I won't know how to act, Will. You should have warned me."

"Baby, it's just James and Patty and besides, he never bragged about his money. I had no idea." He squeezed her hand. "It's going to be fine. Don't worry."

James opened the door and greeted both Will and Merry with a hug. "Here, let me help you with those." He took one of the suitcases Will was holding. "Come on in. Glad you guys made it safe and sound." He started walking to the staircase and slowed down, remembering his brother's wartime injury. "You need me to take that, Will?"

"No, I got it. I'm getting used to stairs. Took me a while though. Thanks for asking."

"Good to hear, bro. If I had a bedroom down here, I'd give it to you but we don't."

"Aw, we'll make it work just fine, won't we babe?"

Merry was still looking around and missed the question. Will shrugged his shoulders and James laughed. "It can be a little daunting. I don't mean for it to be presumptuous, but I'm forever entertaining clients and I have to portray a certain image, if you know what I mean."

"She'll come back to earth eventually." Both men laughed together, and it felt good.

James opened a door close to the curving staircase and set the luggage inside. "Here you go. This will be your room for the next two weeks. If you need anything, just let me or Patty know. We do have a lady who comes in each day to keep things up around here and she knows where most everything is too, so if she can be of help, she will."

He stepped outside the door. "Dining room is downstairs to the left of the staircase. I believe dinner is almost ready. Come down when you get settled and we'll eat."

It only took a few minutes for Will and Merry to settle in. They entered the dining room hand in hand just as Patty turned from the side-serving table. Merry saw Patty's obviously pregnant stomach and stopped in her tracks, her heart breaking from being barren. The very sight of her sister-in-law pregnant sent her over the edge. She couldn't stop the tears.

"I'm so sorry." She hugged Patty. "Please forgive me. I am happy for you, I really am."

"No, it's me you should forgive. I should have warned you before you came. It's my fault."

"No, having a baby is nothing to apologize for. It just surprised me, that's all. And with everything we're going through, I just felt sorry for myself for a minute. I'll be okay." Merry looked at the sideboard. "Wow, this looks great. Thank you for letting us stay with you. It means a lot to us."

Patty gave her another hug. "What do you mean? You're family. Of course you can stay with us. Anytime. Come on, let's make a plate. I'm hungry."

Will and James pulled chairs out for their wives and all four sat down. Will took Merry's hand and quickly said grace over their meal.

James and Patty respectfully waited for Will to finish then began their meal.

Merry took a bite of her homemade macaroni and cheese. "Oh, this is delicious. Do you think your cook will share the recipe?"

"We can always ask." Patty took a bite. "It is good, isn't it?"

"When are you due?"

"Not till the end of October. I have four months to go. But, so far so good."

"Have you started on the nursery yet? I'd love to see it if you have."

"Would you like to do some shopping with me? We could arrange it around your appointments?"

Merry swallowed hard. Even though envy was clouding her every thought, she realized this baby would be part of her family too. Her very own niece or nephew. "I'd love to." She looked to Will. "Is that okay with you?"

"Of course. You ladies have a great time. That will give me and James a chance to catch up."

The next couple of days were spent catching up and sightseeing. Both Will and Merry loved seeing Houston, especially the Gulf of Mexico. Merry felt like she could stand and stare at the ocean all day. They had gotten up early so they could watch the sun rise over the ocean. She took Will's hand. "How can anyone say there is no God? After seeing this, how can there be any doubt?"

Will quoted one of his favorite verses in response. "For the invisible things of him from the creation of the world are clearly seen, being understood by the things that are made, even his eternal power and Godhead; so that they are without excuse. Romans 1:20 tells us that none of us will have a suitable excuse when we stand before him."

"I'm scared Will. Tomorrow's our appointment. What do you think is going to happen?"

He turned to face her and cupped her chin in his hand. "Whatever happens is in God's hands. No matter what, we will glorify him and trust him to work all this out for his glory. Remember, not our will but his be done." He bent down and kissed her. "Okay?"

She nodded her head, not trusting herself to speak.

Together they walked back to James' car and got in the back seat. Patty's parents were expecting them for breakfast. It was time to get going.

The next morning Will and Merry were seated in a nicely decorated sitting area, waiting for Patty's turn in the doctor's office. "You ready for this?"

"Ready as I'll ever be I guess."

A nurse entered the waiting room with a clipboard in her hand "Merry Jackson?"

Merry squeezed Will's hand and leaned down so only he would hear her. "Pray for me, okay?"

"You know I will." Will watched his wife being led away, wishing he could be with her to hold her hand and support her. He picked up a magazine and tried to occupy himself. He had no idea how long this examination would take, afterward they were to meet with the doctor to discuss Merry's options, if there were any. He prayed she could handle whatever news the doctor had for them. He feared she was going to be heart broken.

Finally, the nurse arrived and called him back. He entered the doctor's office where Merry was already sitting and waiting. She didn't look upset yet so maybe there was hope.

He pulled the chair away from the desk so he could extend his leg and sat down next to his wife and together they waited for the doctor.

"How did it go?"

She shrugged her shoulders. "He examined me and could tell I'd had an abortion, but he didn't say anything one way or the other." She nervously looked toward the door. "I guess we'll find out soon enough."

Will glanced around the room at the framed documents on the wall confirming this doctor was everything he said he was. Well, if there was anyone who could help them, he was their man. And if there was anyone who could put an end to this monthly misery he went through, it was this man.

The man that walked through the door was not what Will expected. He was young, probably in his mid thirties or so and had thick blond hair that extended well past his collar. He was not what one would consider the poster boy for the word doctor, especially a specialist.

Will stood and extended his hand. "Hi, I'm Will Jackson."

The tall lanky doctor accepted his hand. "Dr. Grady" Then nodded toward Will's vacated seat. "Please, make yourself comfortable."

"I'm afraid I don't have good news. After a thorough examination, Merry, short of a divine miracle you will never be able to have children."

Merry felt her stomach flip and ran for the bathroom. Will started to follow but a nurse was already at her side and going into the women's bathroom, so he returned to the doctor's office to wait.

"I'm sorry, Mr. Jackson. I know it's hard to accept, but the ill performed abortion has left her barren. She must have had a partial hysterectomy after the abortion. If Doc had told me about that, I would not have wasted your time."

Will swallowed hard. "Doc didn't know. Merry didn't want anyone to know what she had been through. It's not his fault." He looked toward the hall not wanting Merry to hear what he was about to say. "I think she convinced herself that a mistake had been made, that someone would find a way for her to have the children she desires. In my heart of hearts, I already knew. I thought maybe if she heard it from a specialist, she'd believe it."

"I'm sorry I don't have better news. Have you discussed the possibilities of adoption? Many couples are finding fulfillment through adding to their family through this route."

"No, I think we needed to deal with reality before we could make plans like that. It will be something we discuss though." Will stood up. "I better go and see about Merry. Thank you for taking the time to meet with us. I appreciate it."

Dr. Grady rose as well. "I'm sorry it couldn't be under better circumstances. Please tell Doc hello for me. He is a good friend of my father's, as well as to me." The doctor walked Will to the door then left him to find the ladies bathroom.

Will could hear the sobbing from where he was standing in the hallway. *Blast it all! I'm going in after her!* He slowly opened the door and peeked in. "Merry, honey, can you come out here?"

"Nuh uh"

He made sure no one was watching and slipped in through the open door. She was locked in a stall. "Babe. Come on. We knew this could happen. I want to be here for you. You need to come out and let me hold you. We're in this together, remember?"

"Oh Will. Why would God let this happen?"

His wife's pain was breaking his heart. "Come on, Merry. Open the door."

He heard the sliding mechanism and saw her tear streaked face and found himself sobbing. He pulled her close. "Honey, I'm so sorry."

Together they made their way out into the bright Houston sunshine. Not even the weather felt sympathetic.

"Come on, let's get back to James' place."

Merry wordlessly climbed into the front passenger seat and Will closed the door behind them. Will silently prayed as he drove back to his brother's house.

Lord, please give us back everything the enemy has stolen. Lord, I ask that Merry remember the good things you have provided for us, that you saved her life when she could very well have died. Lord, bring us peace. In the midst of our pain, help us to remember your mercy and grace. Lord, bring healing to both of us and father I ask that you strengthen our relationship through all we are going through. Please don't let a wedge be driven between us.

When Patty met them at the front door Merry just shook her head and her tears fell fresh. Patty took her by the hand. "Come on, honey, let's go get some tea. We need to have a good talk."

Will stood and watched his wife being led away from him for the second time that day. He would never understand women. He turned in search of James. His brother would have the right words.

In the end, there weren't words to help. Nothing could help but time and God's grace. Will and Merry decided to leave a couple of days later. It wasn't fair to bring such great sorrow into a house that was filled with joy, at least as far as Will and Merry knew. Nor did Merry want the constant reminder of seeing her pregnant sister-in-law knowing she would never have the privilege of feeling her own little one growing inside her. Instead of driving directly home, to a house that would never be filled with the sound of children's laughter, they decided to take their time and stay a couple of days by the ocean. Both of them needed to just hold each other and spend time with their Lord. The small Inn they found was perfect. No other soul knew where they were. They had each other and God. At that moment, they needed nothing else.

Chapter 16
Jessi

Jessi picked up all the used tissues and took them to the trash. Even though she knew what her aunt had gone through as a teenager, she didn't know how difficult it was for her afterward. "Aunt Merry, I can't imagine what you went through."

"Yes you can baby. You know exactly what I felt like. When you lost Ethan, did Olivia take his place?"

"Of course not."

"Then you know exactly what I felt like. I was mourning for each and every child I had dreamed of having. You may of only lost one, but the hurt is the same. A mom would gladly give her life for her child and I was no exception."

Jessi started crying all over again. There were some things about her family's past that just hurt, and this was one of them. She felt her aunt's full arms pull her into a hug. "Honey, I didn't tell that story to make you sad. It's just part of the story, part of your story. You had to know. We were all in a bad place. Sometimes life isn't fair. Sometimes it hurts. But God is always faithful and He always has a plan. Even if we don't understand at the time. He is working like only God can, through every tear, every torn heart and every shred of pain. His will was accomplished. And like every other young person, I had to learn the hard way."

Jessi just nodded. She knew her aunt was referring to her own stubborn ways. She still didn't understand but she was willing to listen. If God could use her in spite of her downfalls, then maybe she owed her dad that much, to listen with an open mind and at least offer forgiveness.

Chapter 17
James

James went to Europe alone. Not exactly what he was planning, but sightseeing with a woman who was seven months pregnant didn't exactly sound like fun either. He didn't like traveling without Patty. He supposed he'd have to get used to it. In many societies, a wife on your arm was a clincher for signing major deals. Of course, after James explained his wife's condition, smiles were revealed and papers were signed. Every family minded businessman understood a wife in the family way. He would thank her for it if he thought she would take it well. Unfortunately, she didn't take things well these days. She was beyond emotional.

Another month and maybe she'd get back to normal, if there were such a thing as normal when one had a baby. He had no idea. His only experience with mothers and babies had been his own mother and she was run ragged. Of course, she had a few more babies than he and Patty would have.

He tossed his briefcase into the waiting car, ready to go home. He'd been gone just over a month. He had called to check up on her several times. While she was miserable in the heat, she was doing fine. Her mother had checked up on her as well, as had several friends. He hadn't talked with her during this last week, but all assured him she was in good hands. He may not have approved of having this child, but he did love his wife.

His driver unloaded his bags while he went in search of his wife. Lola, the woman who helped Patty keep up with the place, caught him before he wandered too far.

"Mr. Jackson, your wife is at the hospital. I think she is having the baby."

"It's not time yet."

"Sometimes things happen this way. It's okay. She'll be fine."

James had his driver take him. He was too nervous to drive. As soon as the car pulled up in front of the hospital, he jumped out and ran in. He had not attended any classes with her, or gone for any hospital visits. It seemed foolish now that he had no idea where she was. He looked for the maternity ward on the list of departments but he couldn't see straight. He asked the first person he saw, a candy stripe.

"Excuse me. My wife is having a baby. Where is she?"

"Sir, the maternity ward in on the fourth floor."

He didn't wait for further instructions. He ran for the elevator.

James was sitting in the waiting room with Patty's mom when they got the news. He had a daughter. He still wasn't sure how he felt about that. But, he had to see his wife, to make sure she was all right.

The nurse led him to her room. The baby had been taken to the nursery and he was told he could go see her after he saw Patty. He supposed it wouldn't hurt.

He stood in the doorway watching her sleep. Her blond hair was splayed across the pillow. She had a light bead of perspiration on the bridge of her nose and her dark eyelashes were resting against the gentle rising slope of her cheeks, almost as if she were smiling in her sleep. He had never seen his wife look so beautiful. He had no idea being a mother would affect her like this. He quietly went to her and she slowly opened her eyes. "We have a baby girl."

"I heard." He took her hand. "I hear you did a wonderful job."

"She's beautiful."

"If she looks anything like you, then she'd have to be."

She didn't have the energy to be surprised. "Have you seen her yet?"

"No, they have her at the nursery, getting her all fixed up. She was small. Only six pounds."

"But healthy."

James had to agree. "Yes, she's healthy."

"Can we name her Jessi, after my grandmother?"

"I like that name."

"Me too." She closed her eyes once more. "Now go see her."

"I wanted to see you first, to make sure you are all right."

She smiled, melting his resistance. "I'm fine. Go see your daughter."

"Okay, but I'll be right back."

She was already resting, that smile firmly in place.

He found the nurse and she led him to the nursery. After indicating which baby was his, the nurse working with her brought her to the window. She was the very image of his wife. Soft blond wisps of hair were sticking up everywhere and dark lashes rested against her cheeks. He nodded his head, indicating to the nurse he was finished and went back to see his wife.

He softly whispered to his sleeping wife. "You're right. She is beautiful. She looks just like you." He could have sworn her smile grew a little bit, but then he might have been imagining it.

He kissed her cheek then headed to the waiting car. The whole way home he went back and forth between the two images etched into his memory. One was his wife's smile. The other was a newborn baby girl who was not supposed to have any affect whatsoever on his heart.

* * * *

Life at the Jackson household found its own routine rather quickly. James traveled and met with clients and Patty took care of the baby. On occasion they saw one another in passing. True to her word, Patty took care of Jessi. She was exhausted and more than once, James offered to hire a nanny but Patty refused. She wanted to be her mother, to experience everything that entailed and she didn't want any one else taking her place. The problem was, Patty was beyond tired. She needed some rest and she needed it soon.

They had both managed to go to bed at the same time. James had patiently waited for some alone time with his wife while she had been healing and resting and taking care of Jessi. In the nursery, the baby was sleeping soundly. She was six weeks old and finally getting into a bit of a routine, sometimes. He lay facing his wife. He kissed the top of her nose, then each eye. Somehow motherhood made her more beautiful than he'd ever expected. "You're so beautiful."

She stifled a yawn. "I'm such a mess but thanks for being sweet."

"No, you've never been more beautiful to me than you are right now." He wrapped her in her arms and gently showed her just how beautiful she was. It seemed no matter how far apart they were in distance, or how busy they were in the same location; they found time to carve out for one another. Being close, being intimate kept them in touch with each other and clinging tightly to the love they shared.

Later, as he held her in his arms and she made soft mewing noises reserved for those times she slept

111

deeply, he thought about all they had been through, gone through to get to where they were. He hadn't arrived yet, that was for certain. But, he was a long way from where he had begun on that beaten down farm in Oklahoma. He felt something warm and wet on his arm and realized his wife was drooling. If only she could see herself now, drooling and making her little cat sounds, she'd be appalled. She was always so put together, so refined. Sleep destroyed all attempts at maintaining one's dignity.

He unwrapped himself from around her and was about to turn over when he heard the baby from down the hall. Patty didn't move an inch. He could do this.

He approached the squalling baby and gently removed her from her crib. "Come on little one. Let's go fix you a bottle." He had watched Patty do this many times, sure that if he could make million dollar deals he could feed a baby.

He quietly descended the stairs, trying to keep the little one quiet as he passed his closed bedroom door. He did not want his wife waking up.

Finally, he was standing in front of the open refrigerator. There was a bottle prepared, he would just have to warm it up. The pan of water was still on the stove so he set the bottle in it and turned on the flame. "Can't get it too hot, can we? Wouldn't want to burn your little mouth."

He tested the yellowish fluid on his wrist as he'd watched his wife do many times then went to the rocker to feed his daughter for the first time.

At first he just held the bottle and she sucked greedily. Then, after she became somewhat sated, she paused and stared at him. He stared back, not sure what she was looking at. "And what are you looking at little one?"

As he held her, realization took a firm hold of him and shook him like a tree in a hurricane. She was helpless. She could do absolutely nothing on her own. Anxiety rose up within him as he thought back to his own upbringing. He was unsuitable for this. He would be just like his father and fear that he would ruin this child's life banished all reasonable thinking from his mind. It would be better to work harder and longer to provide for her than to destroy her like his father had almost done to him. He couldn't risk her, he found he loved her too much to even take the chance. He held her perfectly formed fingers in his and rubbed his fingers across her soft cheek. These moments before she grew and found out what a miserable father he was would have to last him a lifetime. He would not risk losing her. He couldn't. He finished feeding her and burping her then held her close. "I love you. I love you so much. I hope someday you understand just how much. I'm protecting you; I'm protecting you from myself. I want to give you everything but I can't allow myself to hurt you and I know I would."

He carried her upstairs to the nursery and changed her diaper and rocked a while with her. Before long she was sleeping soundly and he returned to his own bed. Tears filled his eyes. He was too afraid of failure to try and he knew it. Better to be safe than sorry.

Chapter 18
Jessi

"Mom, didn't he know I'd rather of had him than anything else? Did he really think that money and things would be more important to me than his love? How could he think that?"

"Honey, I don't know. I was so caught up in him letting me have you, I refused to question his fathering skills. I was too afraid he'd make me give you up. You quickly became my life. I liked our life the way it was and I didn't want it to change. I'm sorry. I now know I should have done something, tried to make him interact with you. But, I liked having you to myself. I had no idea that things were going to get worse, that your father was consumed with keeping you protected. Your first few years were the happiest days of my life. You and I spent every waking moment together. We'd go on picnics and to the beach. You loved life. And you loved animals. I'll never forget the day we came home with a puppy. Your father didn't say a word. Not a single word. He looked up from his paper, raised his eyebrows then returned to his paper."

Patty gave her daughter time to swallow all she had heard so far. "We did so much together. We spent more time at the zoo than anyone else I knew. We ended up getting season tickets. I loved it. I treasured every minute we spent together."

The fall you turned four is when our life went crazy. I was content. Your father was content. And you were thriving. Yes, you questioned why he was so distant, but you accepted that this was our life. You had everything you ever desired, dolls and dollhouses, puppies and kittens, although the cats had to stay outside since your dad was allergic to them. You loved to shop for dresses and had a whole closet full of them. You had everything. We spoiled you, probably too much. But you never acted like a brat, I can say that for you."

Jessi was pensive. "I remember being a princess. One memory is really vivid. I was twirling in front of a mirror, watching myself and I twirled so much I fell down."

"That was the day of your recital. You started taking ballet when you were three and had your first recital when you were four. You loved how you looked in your ballerina outfit. You always wanted to wear it."

"Yes, that is it. I vaguely remember wanting to be a ballerina. And you took me to see the nutcracker. I remember."

"Your first live play. You did so well. I was afraid you'd be bored to death but no, the music and the dancing mesmerized you. In fact, you didn't want to leave. You cried when it was over."

You had the birthday party every little princess would want. All your friends came. You wore the prettiest pink dress and we had a giant layered cake decorated in white and pink. And your gift, you went crazy when we gave it to you."

Jessi interrupted. "My pony. That was the year I got a pony."

"Yes, you had begged and begged. I tried to keep you from bothering your father too much, but every chance you got you would sneak into his office. That was when you learned that, even though your father didn't outwardly show you any affection, you really did have him wrapped around your little finger. You begged him for a pony. You had no idea that you had only to ask once and it was yours."

Patty stood up to stretch. "Our life was perfect. I had everything I wanted. Oh, there was room for improvement, but I knew in time as you grew and insisted your father spend time with you, he would. He couldn't deny you anything, so it was only a matter of time. You had no reason to fear him. He never raised his voice to you. He never disciplined you. I had that job. And he gave you everything you wanted. Every little girl's dream."

She swallowed hard. "Then the bottom fell out."

Chapter 19
James

James walked through the front door calling out Patty's name. "Patty, Patty. Where is Jessi?"

It wasn't often Patty heard such desperation coming from her husband. She hurried into the hallway and looked down over the upstairs banister. "Honey, she's at mom's. What's wrong?"

"I need to see her. I need to know she's okay."

"Okay, let me grab my purse. We'll head over there." Patty noticed her husband's shaking hands. "Do you want me to drive?"

"Yeah, sure. But please, hurry."

She started the car and drove as fast as she could without giving any officers cause to pull her over. "Will you tell me what's going on?"

"Do you remember the Martins? The ones with the seven year old son?"

"Yeah, I think so. Didn't we have them over a few months ago? You were working on some kind of deal, right?"

"Yes, that's them. Their son was kidnapped."

"What?" Patty started to drive off the side of the road and yanked hard on the steering wheel to straighten back out. "When?"

"Earlier this morning. Apparently Bradley was on his way to school when the chauffeur was forced to stop. Bradley was taken at gunpoint. They haven't heard from the kidnappers as of yet. The FBI is at their house waiting for the phone call."

"Oh my gosh. Oh, James." Patty stepped on the pedal, not caring if she did get pulled over. She wasn't going to stop until they reached her parent's house. She had to see her baby.

Patty barely had the car stopped and James was already running for the front door. He noticeably slowed down as he approached the door. Certainly everything was okay and he didn't want to scare anyone. Patty caught up with him and let herself in. She yelled out. "Mom, hey, it's me and James."

Her mom stepped out of the dining room. "Oh, well hi. I didn't expect to see you today. Jessi and I are having tea. Want to join us?"

Patty felt her heart begin to slow down when she was able to physically touch her daughter. After hugging her close she replied. "Yeah, I'd like that." Patty briefly took her mother aside to explain what happened while James took a seat opposite where

Jessi sat. *Why am I always tongue tied with my own daughter?*

"Daddy, do you want some tea?"

"Um, yes, I would like that." She poured and he picked up the cup trying to hold onto the miniscule handle with his oversize fingers. He took a sip from teacup. "Mmm, this is very good tea."

"Thank you, daddy."

"Are you having fun at grandma's house?"

"I am. She bought me a new doll. She's sitting next to you. She likes tea too."

James looked at the little blond baby doll sitting on the oversize dining room chair. "Yes, she does seem to like tea."

Patty stood over her husband and placed her hands on his shoulders. "Honey, mom said she won't let Jessi out of her sight. I think we should let her stay now that we know she's safe."

James expressed concern, but wanted to talk with Patty about the idea he was throwing around so having her undivided attention would be a good thing. They left their little girl in the capable hands of Patty's mom and went for a cup of coffee.

James was fiddling with his cup and saucer. He was nervous and that wasn't like him. He wasn't sure Patty was going to like his idea. "I think we need to move. I want to move somewhere safer."

"What? James, I think you're over reacting a little bit."

"Really? You really think so? So, it doesn't bother you that Bradley got abducted on his way to school? The same school that we enrolled Jessi in for next year? It doesn't scare you that someone is

121

targeting a rich family through their young innocent child?"

Patty closed her eyes. Of course Jessi was enrolled at the same school. It was a very well known private school that most families could never afford. "I hadn't thought of that. I will do anything to keep her safe, you know that."

"Then we need to think about relocating. I'm thinking Oklahoma. We'd still be by family and we could set up an office there as well as keep the warehouse office by the docks. It could work Patty." He watched her, trying to figure out what she was thinking. "When Fred and Barbara were killed in that car accident a couple of years ago, I inherited the business, so we could do this no problem. I've thought this through. We can maintain a low profile in Oklahoma. Live reasonably and give no one reason to target us."

"You really have thought this through, haven't you?"

"I can't stop thinking about it. I don't know what I'd do if something happened to one of you because of me."

"Should we take a trip, go see Will and Merry? We haven't gone up to see them in the last couple of years."

"Yeah, let's do it."

Chapter 20
Jessi

"Is that why we moved to Oklahoma? I remember bits and pieces from before we moved, like having a picnic by the ocean and going on boat rides."

"Yes, that was the only reason. Your father was so afraid something would happen to you."

"Did the Martins get their boy back?"

"No, they didn't. They never did find him. That was the deciding factor for us. We lived such a high profile life in Houston and we knew we couldn't hide you entirely, but we could do better in making our lives more private."

"That is so sad. I can't imagine always wondering if one of my children were dead or alive.'

"It was sad. It still is. Their whole family was torn apart. Mrs. Martin ended up in a mental health facility. She was possessed with finding her son. I couldn't blame her, I would have been too."

Jessi pondered everything she had been told thus far. "So much can happen in a lifetime. Every one of us has had our share of heartaches. But we've also experienced great joy in our lifetimes too." She looked first at her mother and then her aunt. "It's easy to look at someone's life and make judgments, especially when it affects you. I understand more now, more than I ever did. But I still can't understand why you and daddy didn't want me." She turned her attention to Merry. "It's not that I'm not grateful Aunt Merry, I am. I love you so much. You mean everything to me. But mom, I guess I'd still like some answers. Most parents raise their own children. They don't give them away to someone else, even family."

Patty knew this was coming. Explaining the beginning was the easy part. How do you tell your child it was just easier? No other explanation. She would never have the relationship she desired with her daughter if she didn't tell her everything. Even then, she might not ever be as close to Jessi as she longed for. Better to tell the truth now than have it turn around and bite you later. "We were in Oklahoma City by your fifth birthday."

Chapter 21
James

James took one last walk through of the new house before he signed on the dotted line. This is the house Patty chose and he had to admit, it would work beautifully. Furthermore, the house was only 15 minutes from Will and Merry's place, which would prove handy when he and Patty had to travel. And from the looks of it, that might be often. Already there were problems at the office in Houston. He thought his employees would handle things better than they were. He'd have to take care of that straight away if this was going to work.

He took his wife's hand. "You're sure this is the one? It's not as big as our house in Houston."

"Honey, the purpose of this move was to be more discreet. We want to blend in more, be less conspicuous."

"Very true. I guess I got used to living large."

"This is the house, James. Let's figure out what we're moving here and what we're getting rid of. I want to get settled. Jessi will be starting school soon."

The realtor was patiently waiting for James to make the deal legal. "Alright then, here goes." He signed the counter offer from the buyer and handed her a deposit check. "I think this should do it."

* * * *

James and Patty climbed the steps to the big Victorian house Will and Merry were renovating. He turned to his wife. "Do you think she'll want to stay for the week?"

"I'm guessing so. She and Merry really hit it off. Gives Merry someone to dote on."

"Well, hopefully Merry will keep her. It would make things easier for the move."

Patty rang the doorbell. "Oh, that's a given. She has already told me any time we need childcare she's available."

"That's good to know." Will opened the door and invited them in. James took a deep breath. "Something smells good."

Merry poked her head from around the kitchen door. "Spaghetti. I hope you're hungry."

"Starved. Buying a new house is hard work. Really makes a guy work up an appetite."

Will smirked. "I wouldn't know about that. Buying this house gave me indigestion."

Merry hit him with a dishtowel. "Stop. You know you love this house."

Patty knelt down by Jessi and whispered in her ear. "Would you like to stay with Aunt Merry while we go and get our things?"

Jessi's eyes grew big. "Yes, can I?"

Merry set the spaghetti sauce on the table. "Can I what?"

Jessi jumped up. "Can I stay with you while mommy and daddy go get our stuff?"

"Of course you can, baby girl. We're going to have so much fun."

* * * *

Over the course of the next year, Jessi spent just as much time at her Aunt Merry's house as she did at home. Uncle Will built her a playhouse in the back yard. She had her own room and got to have a say in how it was decorated. It was really a win-win situation for everyone involved. Patty got to travel with James more and Merry had the little girl she'd always dreamed of having. It was more than she had dared to hope for.

As far as Jessi was concerned, she had the best of both worlds. She got to spend lots of time with her favorite aunt. As long as she eventually went home, she wasn't too concerned with how long she stayed.

As time passed, Patty started traveling with James more and more. Before anyone realized it, Jessi was only going home on the weekends her parents were actually home. Jessi grew despondent and developed an attitude toward her aunt. Patty and

James were now traveling extensively and were often out of the country. It was easier for everyone for her to stay with Will and Merry, that is, easier for everyone except Jessi.

James loved traveling with his wife. It was the life he'd always dreamed of. They traveled all over the world. They saw every major site there was to see. Neither of them thought about the damage they were doing to their daughter. She had always been so independent, so sure of herself. She was growing up and they felt her dependency upon them was weaning.

Neither had any idea how much trouble Jessi was giving her aunt. Had Merry spoke up, something might have been done. The last thing Merry wanted to do was call attention to Jessi's behavior. She finally had her little girl and she would handle it. She wasn't going to lose the only child she would ever have.

Jessi grew out of her rebellious stage and transferred her anger from her aunt and uncle toward her parents. Patty didn't see her hostility until it was too late. She had let things go too far and she lost her daughter to her sister-in-law.

Chapter 22
Jessi

Patty was openly weeping. "I'm so sorry, Jessi. It's my fault. I knew what we were doing was wrong, but I let it go on. It was easier."

Jessi had a hard time emotionally connecting to her mother. It wasn't that she wanted to let her hurt, she just didn't know what to do to make things better. She was willing to forgive, it was just hard to forget.

Merry reassuringly put her hand on Patty's shoulder. "It wasn't all your fault. You had company in taking the easy way out. I was selfish. I wanted your daughter and I had her, even though she was the one paying the price, I got what I wanted." Merry continued. "No, this comes down to all of us. Will tried to tell me many times what our actions were doing to our little girl; I just wouldn't listen to him. I had to have my own way." Merry took Jessi's hand. "I'm sorry too. I have even more to apologize for. I let you blame your mother and father all those years. I should have set you straight." She started crying. "I was just so afraid I'd lose you."

Jessi hugged her aunt close then released her. "You'll never lose me." She pulled her knees up to her chest and rested her chin. Her tears were spilling over.

"Mom, did dad ever regret handing me over to Uncle Will and Aunt Merry?"

"In the end. You see, it was never about what he wanted. In fact, he preferred having you at Aunt Merry's. He thought you would be safer there. He didn't consider your emotional well being, he was most concerned with your physical safely. He was so afraid he'd be just like his father and hurt you. He convinced himself that he wouldn't be a good dad to you."

"So, why did you and dad stop visiting me? I felt like I was abandoned, not loved, and not worthy of your love."

"At first we were just so busy getting the business transferred. We had some employees who quit, who didn't want to relocate and we had to fill in until we found replacements. That is why we initially were leaving you at your aunt and uncle's. Once the business was settled, I had planned on staying home more, being there for you but then the economy took a down swing and I was needed on your father's arm to close more deals. I know, it's not a great excuse, but your father was insistent that the business be prosperous for you, for our grandchildren. He didn't want to leave you in the position his father left him in."

"But, who said I wanted all that? Where did he get that idea? Certainly not from me."

"You see, it wouldn't have mattered what you said. His mind was made up. He chose for you because that is what he would have chosen when he was younger."

"Well, what about later. You stopped coming altogether. Why?"

Patty wiped her eyes with a tissue. "I'm so embarrassed to tell you this because it was my own doing, but I was jealous. I was jealous of your relationship with Merry. You had become her daughter. When I did come around you didn't want anything to do with me. You would ignore me. I know I deserved it, but it still hurt. So, I gave up. I took the easy way out yet again and convinced myself I was too busy and you'd be better off without me."

Jessi stood up and looked out the window. Mark had pulled up and was carrying one sleeping child on his shoulder while the other two were sleepily following behind. Even Olivia's head was drooping. They looked worn out. "Is it possible to love too much?"

Patty walked to her side and put her arm around her. "I know we messed up. I hope you know it was because we are human and not because we didn't love you. The moment I found out I was pregnant with you, I couldn't help but love you." Patty reached for more tissue. "I know we can never get back what we lost. But do you think you might let me in your life, let me be a grandmother to your

131

children? Do you think you can ever forgive me? I'm so sorry, Jessi. I love you so much."

Jessi wrapped her arms around her mother. "Yes, mom, I do forgive you. As much as I love Aunt Merry, I have always wanted, needed my mother. And I still do." She wiped the tears from her cheeks and looked her mother in the eye and tried not to cry. "I wish I could have heard daddy say he loved me just once."

Patty pulled away from her daughter and removed an envelope from her purse. "Here, this is for you. It's from your father."

When Jessi looked up, both her mother and aunt were gone. She sat alone for a long time, praying and seeking peace. She wanted to forgive her parents as well as her aunt and uncle regardless of the wrongs committed but it was hard to erase a lifetime of pain. *Lord, help me to forgive. Help me to be like you.*

Chapter 23
James

Jessi straightened the boys dress shirts and held their hands, trying to keep them quiet. They didn't know their grandfather and their perception of death centered more on playing cops and robbers and killing off the bad guys. As rambunctious as they were, they just didn't sit still for anything. Funeral or no funeral.

Olivia on the other hand had met her grandfather. Besides the fact that she was older, she also was a sensitive compassionate child who contemplated death and its repercussions to a fault. Jessi gladly gave the boys to Mark and took Olivia's hand.

Jessi was surprised the funeral was held in a church. To her knowledge, her father had never accepted Christ. She had anticipated a short service in a funeral home followed by the burial. She wasn't prepared for the message given by the pastor of the church. She looked questioningly to her mother and Aunt Merry, but neither of them looked her way. She would address that later. She looked behind her. Every pew was full. *Who are these people?*

She could hear the boys in the back of the church. "Daddy, I smell food. I'm hungry." The voices grew distant as Mark took them out of the sanctuary.

She concentrated on the words being spoken. "…each of you knew James, some of you were acquaintances, some friends, some business associates and some of you are family. Every one of you had a very different relationship with him. This is not the time to berate yourself for what could have been. This is the time to be thankful for what was and to consider your relationship with others. James and I spoke extensively before he died. He took responsibility for every strained relationship in this room." Jessi looked away from the pastor's direct gaze. It made her uncomfortable that this man, this stranger knew more about her father than she did.

He continued. "He was working on restoring relationships before he died. It gives me great pleasure to tell you the first relationship he restored was his relationship with Christ. That was his first priority. James came to know Christ as a little boy in this very church. We've added on a few rooms since those days, but this altar is where he first knelt to give his heart to Christ. How far we sometimes travel from the faith of our childhood. Some of you have done the same thing. James found himself at this

134

very altar once more when he knelt and gave his life back to the Lord.

"James wanted to tell each of you, don't wait like he did to live right. Don't think you have all the answers. And don't wait until it's too late. Once death comes knocking, there will be no more chances to get right with the Lord.

"In Jeremiah 29:11 God tells us '*For I know the plans that I have for you, declares the Lord, plans to prosper you and not to harm you, plans to give you a hope and a future.*' God does indeed have a plan for your life but how can he accomplish that plan if you won't follow his ways?

"Without Jesus Christ going to the cross there would be no hope. But he did. He died a horrible death so every person ever born would have the opportunity to live eternally with him. Do not squander this gift. It is the greatest treasure you will ever receive. How do you receive this gift you ask? I'll tell you.

"Romans 1:8 through 10 tells us this, '*But what does it say? 'The word is near you; it is in your mouth and in your heart,' that is, the word of faith we are proclaiming: That if you confess with your mouth, 'Jesus is Lord,' and believe in your heart that God raised him from the dead, you will be saved. For it is with your heart that you believe and are justified, and it is with your mouth that you confess and are saved.*'

Jesus made the way."

She could hear the pastor still talking but Jessi tuned him out. The letter was burning a whole in her purse, calling out to her to be read. Soon, she was being led out of the church to the cemetery behind the building.

The servicemen were already graveside when Patty, Jessi, and the rest of the family took their seats. The boys were pointing at the "men with guns" and Mark and Jessi had their hands full in keeping them quiet. The military pallbearers brought her father's casket and placed it on the frame provided. A short graveside message was followed with a lady singing Amazing Grace. Everyone stood for the volley of gunfire and the playing of taps. Patty was presented with the folded flag. The event was so solemn, even the boys knew to be still and quiet. Of course, the warning their father gave them probably had more to do with their good behavior than atmosphere.

Jessi could not cry for a man she barely knew. She prayed her mom didn't expect tears, because she just didn't have them yet. She watched her mother wipe her tears as they lowered the casket into the ground. Her mother threw a rose on the casket. Jessi, Mark, Aunt Merry, and the kids followed suit then made their way back to the church community room where a meal was waiting for them.

Her mother's choice of returning to the simple life her father once knew surprised Jessi. Her father had been all about making a name for himself and making a mark on this world. How ironic he would return to where he came from in this small church of his youth. Some of her aunts and uncles and their families came to her and hugged her. She didn't know these people. She felt out of sorts and out of place. She didn't belong here. She'd always held the opinion that showing up at the funeral when you didn't have anything to do with the living was pointless. Yet, her mother wanted her here. *Now what*? She needed to get away from all this, all these people sharing their condolences. They probably knew him better than she did. She leaned into her husband. "I'm going to slip out and take a walk. I need to be by myself."

He nodded and continued talking with the latest person saying how sorry they were.

Jessi removed the letter from her purse and slipped out the side door unnoticed. She followed the beaten path back to the graveside and took the letter out of its sealed envelope.

Chapter 24
Jessi

My Dearest Jessi,

 Of everything I have accomplished in my life, of everything I have ever taken part in, you are what I am most proud of. I was hoping to tell you these things in person, but alas, time did not permit. Perhaps God had a greater plan in having me pen these words. I have never been a great writer. I have dictated many letters over the years, but written very few. Could it be I finally found my voice in writing of my love for my daughter? Could it be that you would need proof of my love, to assure yourself through the years that your father indeed did love you?

I cannot say, but I would like to think that these words would reassure you that my love for you was more extravagant than words can express. I know I have a funny way of showing it. For that, I ask your forgiveness.

I do not wish to make excuses for my behavior. I do wish to offer you an explanation, as my heart, though misplaced, was well intentioned.

From the moment I first laid eyes on you, I recognized my own inadequacies as a man and as a father. I felt fear rip through me as though my heart had been torn in two. When your tiny fingers grasped mine, when you reached through all my armor with one penetrating glance, you left me defenseless. You were so helpless.

You were almost a month early and I came face to face with your dependency. You needed your mother and me for everything. I have never had anyone need me as much as you did, and I panicked. I over thought my role as your father and I was so afraid of failing, of hurting you. I measured myself against my own father and I found myself fearful of becoming him. In my eyes, nothing could have been worse. And I vowed to never be like him.

At that point, my goal was to always make sure you were provided for. I never wanted to see you lacking. I have come to realize that by not trusting God, and thinking I could accomplish his job much better than he could, I missed out on having the relationship that he intended for us from the start. And I robbed you of having a father that would emotionally show you his love, not just provide for you in love.

As you grew, my need for you grew and while I still maintained my misguided opinions, I found myself unable to stay away. I was there. You didn't see me, but I was there. I was there for your first dance recital. I saw you physically move the little girl in front of you over so you could see your audience. I was there when you recited your poem in the spring arts festival and the boys made fun of you and made you cry. I was sitting in the audience opening night when you played the lead in Romeo and Juliet, and I watched all the boys who made fun of you in grammar school chase after you in high school. Then I watched as you received honors at your high school graduation. I was so proud of you.

When you graduated from college I was crying. You had accomplished what I had never done, what any one in our family had never done. You were a college graduate with a degree. I was simply in awe of you. You looked so grown up and I wondered where all the years had gone. You were so independent, so sure of yourself. And I knew it wasn't because of me.

The saddest day of my life was when your uncle walked you down the aisle. I understood of course, he raised you. That was when I realized that my greatest fear came true, that I had failed as a father. In spite of all my careful planning, working and providing, I had become my worst nightmare, a father like my own.

When Ethan was born I would stand at the nursery window and stare at him, just like I stood before that window when you were born. I held him once. I showed my id to the nurse and she let me hold my grandson. I've created a memorial in memory of him, for the children who have been involved in accidents that require vast medical attention. Ethan was the first recipient of the Ethan's Charity Fund. The fund was the anonymous donor who paid off the remainder of his hospital and long term facility care bills. Hundreds of families have been helped through Ethan's Charity fund. Your son's name will live on in the hearts of many.

I could go on and on, but that will do us no good. While I was there at those most important times physically, I was not there for you in the ways you needed me. It grieves me now to know that I caused you so much pain. When I came face to face with my own mortality, I finally understood my own father and I forgave him for my perceived failures on his part. As Christ found me forgivable, I also forgave myself. To not forgive myself would have been to negate the very thing he did for me at the cross. It took me many years, but I *finally understood the true love of a father. He loved me so completely, I finally found peace.*

I know you already know God's love and for that I am eternally grateful. Someday we will be reunited and all the hurts and tears will be gone. We will see everything as God intended them to be, and we will see his purpose in everything. In the meantime, I will be enjoying my time with my grandson. Please, give my love to Olivia and the twins and my best to Mark. Tell him I am proud of him and the father he has become.

And finally, my daughter, I want to tell you I love you. I have always loved you. You are worthy of all my love and so much more. You have overcome so much in this life. You are the daughter every father dreams of having.

All my love,
Daddy

Chapter 25
Jessi

"Come on Mark, we're going to be late."

"Jessi, we have plenty of time."

Jessi blew her bangs out of her eyes in frustration. "Well, just hurry, okay?"

"Come here." He pulled his wife to him. "You look beautiful. You are going to do a fantastic job. Quit being so nervous."

"I'm so scared, Mark. I mean, I'm not daddy. I'm not a successful business man who is used to dealing with millionaires all the time."

"Jessi, when they see your heart and hear your story, they are going to melt. Trust me. Just knowing you are the daughter of the man who started the charity will be enough. And if for some strange reason it isn't, when they find out that you are Ethan's mother, they will continue to support the charity. I promise." Mark backed up and whistled at his wife. She was dressed in a formal off the shoulder black gown that took his breath away. Her long blond hair was swept up and she was wearing her grandmother's pearls. She was classically beautiful. "Besides, who could turn down someone as beautiful as you?"

"Mark, ugh." She reached for his bowtie. "Here, let me fix that. It's crooked."

Mark turned his attention to the car door he heard outside. "I believe the car is here for us. You ready?"

Two hours later, after a five hundred dollar a plate dinner she couldn't eat, she stood before a captive audience who was there to hear her speak on the reasons why they should continue giving to a charity her father started. She took a deep breath and began.

"Ladies and gentlemen, I thank you for giving me the privilege of being here with you today. Ethan's charity fund was started by my father, James Albert Jackson ten years ago this month. Many of you are long time supporters. Some of you are partnering with Ethan's Fund for the very first time. Your generosity has given parents peace of mind when they have needed it the most. When my son, Ethan, was in the hospital in a coma, the last thing I wanted to think about was how I was going to pay the bills. Even though I had insurance, the bills were astronomical and I didn't have the means to pay what the insurance didn't cover. I cried tears of relief when I was told an anonymous donor took care of the remainder of the bills. At that time I had no idea that my father had started this fund in honor of his grandson. And I had no idea that my son was the first child to benefit from this fund. I can tell you that every parent you have ever helped is and always will be eternally grateful for what you have done for them. Without you, we would have lost everything.

"Even, as in cases like mine, when our worst fears come true and our children go on before us, your generosity allows us to grieve in private without bill collectors bugging us and with all our utilities on and running. I am happy to report that ninety percent of the children you have supported have returned home to be with their families. Your giving has made the difference in the care they have received and the support their parents were able to provide. From experience I can honestly say you make it possible for us to learn to breathe again and learn to live again.

As the new President of Ethan's Fund, I promise to do my part to keep you informed and to remain accountable to you for every dollar that comes into this organization. I am emotionally vested into this venture and I promise that I will do everything in my power to make sure Ethan's fund continues as it has for the last ten years.

"You have invested over ten million dollars into the lives of families that are hurting in ways I pray you will never comprehend. I believe we can do better than that. I believe your hearts are full of compassion and thanksgiving and that because you have been blessed, you will continue to be a blessing. Because you know every child deserves to live. Every child deserves the opportunity to grow up and become what God intended them to be. And every child deserves another day with those they love, if only to hear the words 'I love you' once more."

The End

Enjoy this excerpt of

Until Forever

Book One

Of the

Women **of** Prayer
Series

By

Darlene Shortridge

Until Forever

Chapter 1

Jessi Jensen watched as her husband rubbed her son's hair, and grinned.

"We'll be fine. Don't worry so much. Go on. I'll even have supper ready for you when you get home."

Jessi couldn't help but show apprehension. After all, Mark had just spent six months in rehab. He hadn't taken a drink in over six months, and he was Ethan's dad, but could she trust him? She had learned the hard way a long time ago that trust was a word she could not use in the same sentence with her husband's name.

Mark walked over and smiled at his wife. "Honey, I'm done with all that stuff. I love you. I love Ethan. There's nothing I would do to risk your love or jeopardize our lives together. Please believe me. We'll be okay. I promise."

Jessi bent down to give her son a hug and kiss. They rubbed noses, and Ethan giggled. "Mommy, you always do that."

"What does it mean, Ethan?" Jessi asked, her eyes shining with the threat of tears. Her love for her child overwhelmed her. She'd never had anything in her life that meant so much to her. Not Blackie, the lab her parents had finally permitted her to have when she was six, nor Miranda, her favorite doll that she took to bed with her each night as a child. Nothing she could have ever imagined or experienced could have prepared her for the love she would pour out for this child.

Ethan looked up with an expression you wouldn't expect from a four-year-old. "It means that I love you and you love me until forever, Mama. Just like Jesus. Right, Mama?"

"Yes, sweetheart. Until forever I will love you. Always remember that, Ethan—until forever." Jessi rose from her place next to her son and managed a half smile for her husband. "Take care of him, Mark. I'll see you around four thirty."

She grabbed her school bag and headed out to a cold car with a feeling of dread. If only she had faith like Aunt Merry and her little Ethan, then maybe this wouldn't be so difficult. She closed her eyes for a brief second and tried to pray. Nothing. It would never change. God didn't help losers like her, and he certainly didn't have time to listen to her whining.

She could see why God loved Aunt Merry and Ethan. Of all the people in the world, these were the two she loved the most. Who wouldn't love them? They were the kind of people who inspired others just by watching them. They didn't have to speak a word. The love within them said it all. One look into their eyes, and a person experienced a sense of peace. Aunt Merry had her wisdom and unconditional love, and Ethan with his wide-eyed wonder and innocence. The sound of pelting ice pulled her out of her reverie.

Great! Freezing rain again, she thought. I'll have to call Mark and tell him if he's going out to be careful. I am so sick of these Oklahoma winters.

She slowly pulled out of the driveway and headed to Roosevelt Elementary School, where she taught a classroom full of third graders. Her mind quickly shifted to the task at hand: making it to school in one piece. Why school hadn't already been called off, she couldn't fathom. "Nothing to do now but keep on going," she muttered to herself. "Tomorrow the sun will be out, and it'll be sixty. Crazy January weather. A couple more miles and I am home free, at least until school is out."

Driving slow did have its advantages, Jessi reminded herself. Lately she was in too much of a hurry to take the time to look at the stately old homes that surrounded her school. Someday she would love to live in a house like one of these—two-story, brick homes with white shutters and brick sidewalks leading up to big front doors with brass knockers; front porches, with porch swings, that spanned the entire front of the house. Some of the homes still had Christmas decorations up. Big, fresh green wreaths with red bows hanging from second-story balconies and candles lit in every window. Even brightly colored lanterns with little tea lights graced the steps to a few of the homes.

One night she had taken Ethan on a Christmas-light drive, and she purposely drove through this neighborhood. She had fallen in love with the lanterns and the candles, all the decorations, really. Something about a candle in a window made a place feel inviting, like you could go in and sit by a fire with a mug of hot chocolate and a good book. The tree would be brightly lit with gifts underneath and a train track running completely around it. Antique glass ornaments of all shapes and sizes would hang from each limb, and an angel would grace the top, watching over her keep. She could still picture the look on Ethan's face as he took it all in. He was in awe over everything. Ethan had his favorites too: the snowmen with eyes of coal and carrot noses, Santas and reindeer on rooftops, and oh, the lights—bright white lights, blue ones, or all the multi-colored sets. He couldn't get enough of them. Some flickered, and some raced along. Faster and faster, just like his race cars at home. He even rounded out the scene with his own sound effects—*zoom, zoom.* What surprised her most was when he wanted to stop the car and get out for a nativity scene. "Mom, please," he'd pleaded, and she'd never been able to deny those eyes when he really put his all into it. They stopped for a little while, and she watched as he went from life-sized camel to cow to lamb. He would stand at each piece for a minute or two. Finally, he ended up at the manger. When he knelt down on his knees and bowed his head, tears formed in her eyes. Normally, she took his faith with a grain of salt, knowing he was a four-year-old boy who was greatly influenced by his great-aunt Merry, who watched him while Jessi was working. This time she did not know why she let this simple act of obedience to a God she refused to serve bother her.

On occasion when Jessi would let herself drift, she liked to think about what others had and what she was lacking. On occasion she became quite maudlin, and she forgot exactly what she had to be thankful for. It usually happened when something in her life was considerably stressful. She would find herself wandering, daydreaming about living in someone else's life or the "once upon a time" dreams she had had and how far away she was from seeing them become a reality.

Maybe this time Mark would be able to stay dry and hold down a job. Her own salary was steady, but it wouldn't allow her to live in a neighborhood like this one or eventually get that great play set Ethan had wanted for Christmas. Money was always just a little too tight. Expectations were always a little too high,

and too many times reality was a bit too much of a
letdown. She'd done her best for Ethan with
Christmas this year. She found him a great
refurbished two-wheeler in the perfect colors: blue
and red. It had tassels hanging from the handlebars
and a horn that he just loved honking. But she wanted
to do more. She'd loved their little house when they
first bought it. She knew it would be a first home, and
she was okay with that. They would fix it up little by
little, and as their family grew, they would move into
something bigger and start the process again and
again until they were in their dream house. Where did
all those dreams go?

*I guess the ice is giving everyone a hard time this
morning*, she thought as she pulled into an empty
parking lot. The only other car was Principal Davies'.
She half skated across the parking lot as she made her
way to the school building. The sound of silence that
greeted her as she walked in the door was altogether
unnatural for a school. At the very least she should
have heard teachers chatting among themselves, chalk
clicking upon chalkboards in preparation for a day of
learning, and the sound of a typewriter emanating
from the office as Julie, the school secretary, typed
memos from her perch behind the counter. Nothing
but silence.

"Hello, is anyone here?" Jessi yelled out, knowing
full well that Dr. Davies was somewhere in the
building.

Not only was his car in the parking lot, but the doors were unlocked. At least the teachers' entrance was.

"Jessi? Is that you?" Dr. Davies rounded the corner, probably coming from the copy room. "Didn't you receive my message? I left a message on your voicemail that school had been cancelled for today. This ice storm is going to be a killer."

Jessi groaned and glanced outside. She had forgotten to charge her cell phone. Her windshield looked like one of those glass block showers. Everything was out of focus. Heading straight home now would definitely be a problem. At the very least, the roads wouldn't be drivable until the rain stopped. She wasn't sure if the city even owned salt or sand spreaders, let alone was able to pay someone enough to risk their lives trying to save someone else's. Probably not.

The words "Looks like I'll be getting caught up on some of my grading today," managed to escape from her lips, when all she really wanted to do was get back in her car and head home. She resigned herself to her day, even though her heart screamed for a second chance. If only she had checked the messages before she and Mark had their semi-argument she would be at home right now having breakfast with her son. If only. Her life thus far had been a series of "if onlys." *If only Mom and Dad had loved each other enough to stay together. If only I had listened to the voices in my past telling me that Mark was nothing but trouble. No, that's not right. Then I wouldn't have*

Ethan, and I would do anything for Ethan…even marry Mark again.

As she entered her classroom, her mental to-do list caught up with her. She made her way to her desk and began to check items off her list. It felt good to be getting something done. With everything else happening in her life, she hadn't been able to keep up with her schoolwork. As she immersed herself in her work, she completely forgot about calling Mark.

***

By eleven, things seemed to be getting a bit better. The freezing rain had changed to rain as the air warmed up a bit. Mark figured this was as good a time as any to head out and grab the ingredients he needed for dinner. "Come on, buddy. We have to run to the store. Where's your coat?"

Ethan went to his hook in the hallway where Mom put his coat and his backpack. He grabbed his coat, which was bright orange (Mom said it was easier to find him in a crowd that way), and walked back to his dad, who helped him put it on. "It shouldn't take us too long. Your mom still likes spaghetti, right?"

"She loves it, especially the cheese bread," Ethan said, speaking more for himself than his mother.

Together they headed out to the garage, where Mark's car had been sitting for the last six months. He still had his license, as his rehab stint hadn't been the result of an accident. He'd willingly checked himself in to prove to Jessi that he didn't have a problem. He figured if he went willingly, she would know he really wasn't an alcoholic, as she so loved to call him. And he'd proved himself. He didn't have a problem. A guy with a problem wouldn't be able to go six months without a beer, right? He couldn't figure out what the big deal was. What was so wrong with a beer now and then? And what was with her attitude this morning. It was like she didn't trust him with his own son. Well, Ethan was his son too, and he had just as much of a right to be with him as Jessi did. As far as he was concerned, she sheltered the kid a bit too much for his own good. If he was going to learn to get along in the real world, he was going to have to be in it once in a while. And besides that, she was going to turn him into a mama's boy. That was out of the question. No son of his was going to be some whining wimp tied to his mama by the apron strings. It was time to take over the education of young Ethan and teach him to be a man.

Mark opened the car door and helped Ethan get buckled in his booster seat. That was one thing he would not challenge Jessi on. She'd blow up if she ever found out Ethan wasn't in his safety seat. Their man-to-man talks would have to be from the front seat to the backseat, not like Mark and his dad's— sitting next to each other in his dad's old Buick, his dad with a beer in his hand, and him with a root beer, just like Dad. *Someday I'll be just like him*, he had thought to himself. He would picture himself sitting in the front seat of a car like this one on a hot summer day with a nice cold beer. Nowadays you couldn't even have a beer outside of the car and then drive, let alone tool along with one. Course, he didn't let laws keep him from having fun when he was younger. He and his buddies would pick up a case and cruise down country roads like there was no tomorrow.

Yep, the fun stopped about six years ago, when he met Jessi. Granted she wasn't a religious freak like her aunt Merry, but she was pretty straitlaced—no partying, no swearing, and certainly no fooling around before they were married. She was up front with him about that. He figured she was lying to him about the religion stuff. It turned out she wasn't. She didn't have time for a God who would allow so much pain and suffering in her life. Then she figured she wasn't worthy of his love anyway. He could never figure that one out. If ever there was someone worthy of God's love, it was a goody-two-shoe like his wife. He had never been attracted to teachers' pets or Ms. Perfects before. She definitely fit into those categories. For the life of him, he could not remember what it was that had attracted him to her in the first place. She was pretty, that was for sure, with her blond hair and dark eyes. Dark brown. He'd never seen such dark eyes before. Indian eyes, she had told him later. He first noticed her at one of the college hangouts near Oklahoma State University. She'd been sitting with her friends at a table, and they were laughing and carrying on, and he couldn't take his eyes off her. He'd asked her to dance, and they danced a couple of numbers before he offered to buy her a beer. She politely declined the beer and asked for a Sprite. He should have figured something was up with that but then dismissed it with the thought she was probably letting up because she was driving. Talk about wrong first impressions. Later he'd learned the only reason she was even there was because it was one of her roommates' birthdays and she was in the minority when it came to choosing the place to celebrate. He'd gotten her number and promised to give her a call. After putting it off for a week, he was unable to get her off his mind, so he called her. They decided to get together the following Saturday for the OSU vs. OU football game. Being big rivals, the game promised to be packed to the hilt and a great showdown between two good football teams. About a half hour before kickoff, Jessi met him outside the stadium, as planned. He was duly impressed by her knowledge of football and didn't mind letting her know. She had played flute in the marching band all through high school and had never missed a game in four years. Sometimes she lost her voice from yelling so much but never missed a game. Therefore, she developed an understanding of football, if not a love of the game.

The next thing he knew it was a year later and they were standing at an altar saying "I do." A year after that, Ethan was born. Everything had been a series of up and downs since then. She had her teaching degree and had no problem securing a job in Oklahoma City, teaching inner-city third graders, while he drifted from construction crew to construction crew. It seemed as though he would just get in a rhythm at one job and then they'd let him go. So he'd been late

161

a few times and had a couple at the local bar with his burger at lunch. Everyone else was doing the same thing. Shoot, a couple of times his crew chief drank one down with him. He still couldn't figure out what the big deal was. Mark jumped when the car behind him laid on the horn. Green light.

Mark pulled into the parking lot of the grocery store, looked back at Ethan, and started to say something when he noticed Ethan was sound asleep in his car seat. *Well, I suppose if I lock the doors he'll be just fine. I just need a couple of things, and I'll only be a minute*, he thought to himself. Mark hurried into the nearly empty store and found the pasta, sauce, and French bread. He bought some cheese and the makings for a salad and then hurried out to where he left Ethan. He found him right where he left him, sound asleep. He wasn't sure if Ethan still took naps, but today he did.

Mark took a different route home, thinking the roads might be a little better than they were on route to the store. He saw the sign before he could really even read it: Pappy's Bar and Grill. And it beckoned him like a lighthouse guiding a lost ship. *I'll just go in and say hi to everyone,* he reasoned with himself. He looked back at Ethan, who was still sleeping soundly, and figured if he was okay in the grocery parking lot he would be fine for a few minutes while he went in to see his friends. He wouldn't drink anything; he'd promised Jessi. He'd just say hi. He got out, locked the doors, and headed straight for the door.

***

Ethan woke up and looked around. He was cold. He let himself out of his car seat and curled up on the backseat of the car with the blanket his mother kept handy for emergencies. He recognized it for its warmth, curled up, and went straight back to sleep on the backseat of the old Buick.

***

It wasn't until lunchtime that Jessi remembered to call home. No answer. She tried calling several times while she ate lunch. Still no answer. She closed her eyes and rested her arms and head on her desk. She breathed deeply, wishing she had remembered to call earlier.

It was something she would never forgive herself for.

About the Author

Darlene Shortridge is the best selling author of three Contemporary Christian Novels. She is an accomplished vocalist and a compassionate speaker. She lives in Oklahoma City with her husband and son. Being a northern gal, she is quite proud of her developing language skills, especially when some dear friends taught her how to properly use the phrase, "Bless Your Heart."

You can visit Darlene at her website - http://www.darleneshortridge.com
As well as connect with her at these places - Facebook
http://www.facebook.com/AuthorDarleneShortridge
Twitter https://twitter.com/#!/ShortridgeD
Blog http://darleneshortridge.blogspot.com/

Made in the USA
Columbia, SC
04 June 2021

38963924R00095